"I have a little confess[...] in closer so only he could hear her words. "This is my first ball."

He looked at her closer, wondering if he had been wrong in assessing her age. It was hard to tell with the mask covering her eyes, but he did not think he had got his estimation wrong.

"I have been to dances. Just not to any balls like this."

"How can that be, Miss James?"

She bit her lip and flicked him a nervous glance.

"If I tell you, you might have me escorted out."

It was his turn to smile.

"I doubt it, Miss James. Unless you tell me you sneaked in with the sole purpose to sabotage Lady Salisbury's ball or steal her silverware."

Miss James pressed her lips together and then leaned in even closer, her shoulders almost touching his.

"You are half right," she said, her voice low. She flicked him an amused glance. "I did sneak in."

Simon felt a swell of mirth rise up, and he realized for the first time in a long time that he was having fun.

Author Note

When my lovely editor asked if I would like to write a book that would be a part of A Season of Celebration, celebrating seventy-five years of Harlequin, I was thrilled. Ten years ago, my first book was published, and it has been a wonderful decade writing for a line of books I had read and admired for a long time before ever putting pen to paper. I have huge respect for the other Harlequin Historical authors and am always excited to see what books are published alongside my own each month.

The Kiss That Made Her Countess starts at a Midsummer Eve ball. I wanted to invoke some of the mystery and magic of Midsummer to create a spectacle that would sweep Alice and Simon along, something so special that they would forget the rules they should follow and the expectations of Society. I hope you enjoy their story and experience some of that Midsummer magic for yourselves.

THE KISS THAT MADE HER COUNTESS

LAURA MARTIN

HISTORICAL

Harlequin® HISTORICAL

ISBN-13: 978-1-335-59624-6

The Kiss That Made Her Countess

Copyright © 2024 by Laura Martin

Recycling programs for this product may not exist in your area.

For questions and comments about the quality of this book, please contact us at CustomerService@Harlequin.com.

TM and ® are trademarks of Harlequin Enterprises ULC.

Harlequin Enterprises ULC
22 Adelaide St. West, 41st Floor
Toronto, Ontario M5H 4E3, Canada
www.Harlequin.com

Printed in U.S.A.

Laura Martin writes historical romances with an adventurous undercurrent. When not writing, she spends her time working as a doctor in Cambridgeshire, where she lives with her husband. In her spare moments, Laura loves to lose herself in a book and has been known to read from cover to cover in a single day when the story is particularly gripping. She also loves to travel—especially to visit historical sites and far-flung shores.

Books by Laura Martin

Harlequin Historical

The Viscount's Runaway Wife
The Brooding Earl's Proposition
Her Best Friend, the Duke
One Snowy Night with Lord Hauxton
The Captain's Impossible Match
The Housekeeper's Forbidden Earl
Her Secret Past with the Viscount
A Housemaid to Redeem Him

Matchmade Marriages

The Marquess Meets His Match
A Pretend Match for the Viscount
A Match to Fool Society

The Ashburton Reunion

Flirting with His Forbidden Lady
Falling for His Practical Wife

Scandalous Australian Bachelors

Courting the Forbidden Debutante
Reunited with His Long-Lost Cinderella
Her Rags-to-Riches Christmas

Visit the Author Profile page
at Harlequin.com for more titles.

To my boys,
everything is so much more fun with you

Chapter One

Northumberland, Midsummer's Eve, 1816

Not for the first time that evening Alice felt ridiculous. She glanced down at the borrowed dress, the hem splattered with mud, and the delicate shoes. If they ever made it to Lady Salisbury's ball she would trail dirt all over the ballroom floor.

'Come, Alice. We can't stop now,' Lydia called over her shoulder before vaulting over a wooden fence. Alice followed a little more slowly, wondering how she had been dragged into this madcap plan. 'We're almost there. I swear I can hear the music.'

With as much grace and elegance as she could muster, Alice climbed over the fence, closing her eyes in horror as the material of her dress snagged on a protruding nail. There was the sickening sound of ripping fabric as she lost her balance and the dress was tugged free.

'Lydia, wait,' Alice shouted, looking up to see her friend plunging head first through a hedge. She had no choice but to follow, grimacing as she spotted the ripped area near the hem of her dress. Hopefully she would be able to mend it and clean it before her cousin even noticed the dress was missing.

She paused before the hedge, wondering how Lydia had made her way through the dense foliage, and then a hand shot out and gripped her wrist. Lydia was giggling as Alice emerged, an expression of surprise on her face, and soon Alice was laughing too.

'Just think, in a few minutes we will be whirling across the ballroom in the arms of the most handsome bachelors in all of Northumberland,' Lydia said as she gripped Alice's hand. 'Maybe there will be a dashing duke or an eligible earl to sweep you off your feet.'

For a moment Alice closed her eyes and contemplated the possibilities. It was highly unlikely she would meet anyone at the ball that could save her from the impending match that made her heart sink every time she thought of her future.

'My last night of freedom,' she murmured.

Lydia scoffed. 'You make it sound as if you are on your way to the gallows.'

'That is exactly what it feels like.'

'Surely he is not that bad.'

Alice screwed up her face and gave a little shudder. 'I am well aware I have lived a sheltered life so have not come across the scoundrels and the criminals of this country, but Cousin Cecil is by far the worst person I have ever met.'

'Perhaps your parents will not make you marry him.'

'I doubt they will save me from that fate.' Tomorrow Alice's second cousin, Cecil Billington, was coming to stay for a week with the single purpose of finalising an agreement of marriage between him and Alice. As yet he had not proposed, but Alice was aware of the negotiations going on in the background with her father. She hadn't dared enquire as to the specifics; even just the idea of Cecil made her feel sick.

'Then, tonight will have to make up for the next forty years of putting up with Cecil.'

Lydia grabbed her by the hand and began pulling her over the grass again. The house was in view now, the terrace at the back lit up with dozens of lamps positioned at equal intervals along the stone balustrade. Music drifted out from the open doors, and there was the swell of voices as those escaping the heat of the ballroom strolled along the terrace.

'Someone will see us,' Alice said, feeling suddenly exposed. There was only about thirty feet separating them and the house now, but it was all open lawn, and by the time they reached the steps leading up to the terrace it would be a miracle if they made it even halfway unobserved.

'Then, let us act like we belong. We more than look the part. If we stroll serenely arm-in-arm, I wager no one will pay us any attention. We are just two invited guests having a wonderful time at the Midsummer's Eve ball.'

Alice considered for a moment and then nodded. 'You are right. If we try to creep in, it will be obvious immediately. The only way we have half a chance is by pretending we are meant to be here.'

Instantly she straightened her back and lifted her chin, trying to mimic the poise and confidence of Lady Salisbury, the hostess of the sumptuous masked ball. Sometimes Alice would catch a glimpse of the viscountess stepping out of her carriage or taking a stroll through the extensive grounds of Salisbury Hall. She looked regal in her posture and elegant in her movements, and Alice tried to copy how she held herself and how she walked.

'Wait,' Lydia called and slipped a mask into Alice's hand. It was delicate in design, only meant to fit over the upper part of the wearer's face. White in colour, it had an intricate silver pattern painted onto it, a collection of swirls and dots that glimmered in the moonlight. Alice put it on, securing the mask with the silver ribbon tied into a bow at the back of her head. She looked over to Lydia to see her friend had a similar mask now obscuring the top half of her face.

Lydia slipped her arm through Alice's, and together they strolled slowly across the lawn. Despite her urge to run, Alice knew this ruse would work best if they moved at a sedate pace. No one blinked as they ascended the stairs onto the terrace, and Alice heard her friend suppress a little squeal of excitement as they reached the doors to the ballroom.

Neither girl had ever been to a ball like this before. On occasion they would attend the dances at the local Assembly Rooms, but even those were few and far between. Once Alice had begged her parents to allow her and her sister to stay with some friends in Newcastle to enjoy the delights of the social calendar there, but worried about their daughters' reputations, her parents had refused.

'This is magical,' Alice whispered, pausing on the threshold to take everything in. The room was large and richly decorated. The walls were covered in the finest cream wallpaper. At set intervals there were large, gold-framed mirrors, positioned to reflect the guests on the dance floor and make the ballroom seem as if it were even bigger than it was. From the ceiling hung two magnificent chandeliers, each with at least a hundred candles burning bright and illuminating the room. In between the mirrors on the walls there were yet more candles, flickering and reflecting off the glass and making the whole ballroom shimmer and shine.

The assembled guests added to the vision of opulence, the men in finely tailored tailcoats with silk cravats and the women in beautiful dresses of silk and satin. The theme of this masked ball was the Midsummer celebrations, and many of the guests had dressed with a nod to this in mind. Some women had freshly picked flowers woven into their hair or pinned to their dresses as they normally would a brooch.

'I have never seen anything like this,' Lydia said, her mouth open in awe.

'Thank you,' Alice said, squeezing her friend's hand. 'For making me come tonight. You're right. I deserve one last night of happiness before a lifetime of being married to vile Cousin Cecil.'

Lydia leaned in close and held Alice's eye. 'Enjoy it to the utmost. Dance with every man that asks, sip sparkling wine like it is water, admire all the marvellous women in their beautiful dresses.'

'I will.'

For a moment Alice felt a little overwhelmed. This was not her world, not where she belonged, and she was aware she didn't know how to talk to these people. It felt as though someone might come and pluck her out of the crowd and announce *Alice James, you do not belong here*.

A young gentleman, no older than Alice and Lydia, approached, swallowing nervously. He smiled at them both, showing a line of crooked teeth, and then directed his focus on Lydia.

'I know we have not been introduced, but may I have the pleasure of the next dance?'

Alice watched as her friend blushed under her mask. Lydia was bold and confident on the outside, but sometimes she would stutter and stammer amongst people she did not know.

'I would be delighted,' Lydia said, giving Alice a backwards glance as her partner led her off to the edge of the dance floor to wait for the next dance to be called.

Suddenly alone Alice felt very exposed, and she shrank back, aghast when she brushed against a large pot filled with a leafy plant with brightly coloured flowers. It wobbled on its table, threatening to crash to the ground. She lunged, trying to steady it, and as her hands reached around the ceramic she had an awful vision of the container crashing to the floor and the whole ballroom turning to her in the silence that followed, realising she shouldn't be there.

'Steady,' a deep voice said right in her ear, making her jump and almost sending the pot flying again. An arm brushed past her waist, reaching quickly to stop the plant from toppling.

For a long moment Alice did not move, only turning when she was certain there was going to be no terrible accident with the plant in front of her. When she did finally turn she inhaled sharply. Standing right behind her, just the right distance away so as not to attract any disapproving stares, was the most handsome man she had ever laid eyes on. He wasn't wearing a mask, and Alice reasoned there was no point. Everyone in the room would know who he was just by looking at his eyes. They were blue, but not the same pale blue of her own eyes but bright and vibrant, piercing in their intensity. He had that attractive combination of blue eyes and dark hair that was uncommon in itself but that, added to the perfect proportions of the rest of his facial features, meant he was easily the most desirable man in the room.

'Thank you,' she said, her heart still pounding in her chest from the worry that she was about to cause a scene with the crashing décor. 'That could have been a disaster.'

Simon smiled blandly at the pretty young woman in front of him and turned to leave, not wanting to get caught up in conversation with someone he should probably know. There were hundreds of young ladies in Northumberland he'd been introduced to, and he could never remember their names. It was one of the tribulations of being an earl: everyone knew you, everyone recognised you, and most expected you to remember them.

His brother had been good at that sort of thing, remembering every face and name, making connections between members of the same families. When out on the estate or visiting the local village Robert would stop and talk to almost everyone he met, enquiring after the health of various ailing relatives or newborn babies. Robert had been loved by their tenants and staff in a way that was impossible to follow, especially when Simon had trouble remembering even a fraction of the names of the people he encountered in the local area.

As he turned he spotted his sister-in-law entering the ballroom. He had a lot of time and respect for Maria, the dowager countess, but right now he did not want to see her. Recently she had been urging him to marry and settle down, which was the furthest thing from what he had planned for his life. Tonight no doubt she would have a list of eligible young ladies lined up for him to dance with, all perfectly nice and decent young ladies, but there was no point in him seeking a connection with anyone, not now, not ever.

Not wanting to get caught by Maria and her list of accomplished young ladies, he hastily turned back to the woman in front of him.

'I don't think we've been introduced,' he said.

'Miss Alice James,' she said, bobbing into a little curtsy. She looked up at him expectantly, and he realised she was waiting for him to introduce himself.

'Lord Westcroft,' he said, seeing her eyes widen. Unless she was a consummate actress it would seem she hadn't known who he was. He didn't like to view himself as conceited, but generally most people *did* recognise him when he entered a room. It was one of the disadvantages of being an earl.

'A pleasure to meet you, my Lord.'

'The dancing is about to begin, Miss James. I wonder if I might have the pleasure of this dance?'

'You want to dance with me?' She sounded incredulous, and he had to suppress a smile at her honest reaction.

'If that is agreeable to you?'

She nodded, and he held out his arm to her, escorting

her to the dance floor just as the musicians played the first note of the music for a country dance.

He had been dancing all his life, and over the years been to hundreds of balls and danced countless dances. Before his brother had died he had quite enjoyed socialising, but everything had lost its shine after Robert's death. Miss James stood opposite him and beamed, looking around her in delight. She was young, but not so young that this could be her first ball, and he wondered if she approached everything with such irrepressible happiness.

The dance was fast-paced, and as it was their turn to progress down the line of other dancers, Miss James looked up at him and smiled with such unbridled joy that for a moment he froze. Thankfully he recovered before she noticed, and they continued the dance without him missing a step, but as they took their place at the end of the line he found he could not take his eyes off her. Even with her mask on he could see she was pretty. She had thick auburn hair that was pinned back in the current fashion, but a few strands had slipped loose and curled around her neck. Her eyes were a pale blue that shimmered in the candlelight, but the part of her he felt himself drawn to was her lips. She smiled all the time, her expression varying between a closed-lip, small smile of contentment to a wider smile of pleasure at various points throughout the dance. When she got a step wrong, she didn't flush with embarrassment as many young ladies would, but instead giggled at her own mistake. Simon realised he hadn't met anyone in a long time who was completely and utterly living in the moment and, in that moment, happy.

As the music finished he bowed to his partner and then surprised himself by offering her his arm.

'Shall we get some air, Miss James?'

She looked up at him, cheeks flushed from the exertion, and nodded.

'That would be most welcome.'

Simon saw his sister-in-law's eyes on him as he escorted Miss James from the dance floor to the edge of the ballroom, stopping to pick up two glasses of punch on the way. The ballroom was hot now, with the press of bodies, and it was a relief to step outside into the cool air.

'I think Midsummer might be my new favourite time of year,' Miss James said as they chose a spot by the stone balustrade. She leaned on it, looking out at the garden and the night sky beyond.

'What has it displaced?' Simon asked.

'I do love Christmas. There is something rather magical about crackling wood on the fire whilst it snows outside and you are all snug inside. But I will never forget this wonderful Midsummer night.'

'Forgive me, Miss James, but have we met before?'

'No.'

'You seem very certain.'

She smiled at him. There was no guile in her expression, and he realised that she had no expectation from him. Most young women he was introduced to looked at him as something to be conquered. Their ultimate aim was to impress him so they might have a chance at becoming his countess. It was tiresome and meant he had started to avoid situations where he was likely to be pushed into small talk with unmarried young women. Miss James had no calculating aspect to her; she was not trying to impress him. It was refreshing to talk to someone and realise they wanted nothing from you.

'I think I would remember, my Lord.'

'You are from Northumberland?'

'Yes, my family live only a few miles away.'

'Then, our paths must have crossed at a ball or a dinner party, surely.'

He saw her eyes widen and a look of panic on her face. He wondered for a moment if she might try to flee, but instead she fiddled with her glass and then took a great gulp of punch.

'I have a little confession,' she said, leaning in closer so only he could hear her words. 'This is my first ball.'

'Your first?'

'Yes.'

He looked at her closer, wondering if he had been wrong in assessing her age. He'd placed her at around twenty or twenty-one. Young still, but certainly old enough to have been out in society for a good few years. It was hard to tell with the mask covering her eyes, but he did not think he had got his estimation wrong.

'I have been to dances,' she said quickly. 'Just not to any balls like this.'

'How can that be, Miss James?'

She bit her lip and flicked him a nervous glance.

'If I tell you, you might have me escorted out.'

It was his turn to smile.

'I doubt it, Miss James. Unless you tell me you sneaked in with the sole purpose to sabotage Lady Salisbury's ball or steal her silverware.'

Miss James pressed her lips together and then leaned in even closer, her shoulders almost touching his.

'You are half-right,' she said, her voice low so only he could hear.

'You plan to steal Lady Salisbury's silverware.'

She flicked him an amused glance. 'No, I am no criminal, but I did sneak in.' As soon as she said the words, she clapped her hands over her mouth in horror. 'I can't believe I just told you that. It was the one thing I was meant to keep secret tonight, and it is the first thing I tell you.'

Simon felt a swell of mirth rise up inside him, and he realised for the first time in a long time he was having fun. Fun had seemed a foreign concept these last few years. In a short space of time he had lost his brother, inherited a title he had never wanted and been forced to confront the issue of his own mortality. He'd been forced into making monumental decisions over the last few weeks, everything serious and fraught with emotion.

'You sneaked in?'

She nodded, eyes wide with horror.

'Are you going to tell anyone?'

'I am not sure yet,' he said, suppressing a smile of his own.

'Lydia is going to be furious,' Miss James murmured.

'There are two of you?'

She closed her eyes and shook her head. 'I need to stop talking.'

'Please don't, Miss James. This is the most fun I've had for months.'

'Now you're mocking me.'

'Not at all.'

'You're an earl. This cannot be the most fun you've had. Your life must be full of luxury and entertainment.'

'I find it is mainly full of accounts and responsibilities,' he said. 'That is unfair and very... I am well aware of the privileged life I lead. It is full of luxury and extravagance, as you say, but not fun.'

'That is sad,' Alice said, and she touched him on the hand. It was a fleeting contact, but it made his skin tingle, and he looked up quickly. There was no guile in her eyes, and he realised the furthest thing from her mind was seduction—whether because she had a young man she fancied herself in love with or because their backgrounds were so far apart she knew there could never be anything between them.

'It is sad,' he said quietly. 'So tonight I charge you with lifting this grumpy man's spirits.'

'And in exchange you will not expose my deception.'

'We have a deal. Tell me, Miss James, how did you manage to sneak in without one of the dozens of footmen seeing you?'

She motioned out at the garden beyond the terrace. Only the terrace was lit, the grass and the formal garden beyond in darkness.

'We crept through the garden.'

He glanced down and laughed. 'I can see there was a little mud.'

'I was terrified when we arrived that I might have foliage in my hair. We had to squeeze through a hedge to get into the right part of the garden.'

'That is commitment to your cause. What made you so keen to come here tonight?'

She sighed and looked out into the darkness.

'I doubt you know the feeling of helplessness, of not being in control of your own future,' she said with a hint of melancholy. She was wrong in her assumption, but now was not the time to correct her. 'Soon I will not be able to choose anything more thrilling than what curtains to hang or what to serve for dinner.'

'You are to be married.'

The expression on her face told him she was not happy about the prospect.

She straightened and turned to face him. 'I am to marry my second cousin, vile Cecil.'

'Vile Cecil?'

'It is an apt description of him.'

'I already feel sorry for you. What makes him so vile?'

Miss James exhaled, puffing out her cheeks in a way that made him smile. He didn't know her exact background, but by the way she spoke and held herself he would guess she was from a family of the minor gentry. Perhaps a landowner father or even a vicar. She knew how to conduct herself but hadn't been subject to the scrutiny many of the women of the *ton* had to endure, so the odd shrug of the shoulders or theatrical sigh hadn't been trained out of her.

'Where to start? Imagine you are a young lady,' she said, and he adopted his most serious expression.

'I am imagining.'

'Good. You are introduced to a distant relative about fifteen years older than you,' she said and held up a finger. 'The age gap is not an issue you must understand. I am aware women are of higher value to society when they are young and beautiful and men when they are older and richer.'

'I did not think you would be such a cynic, Miss James.' Simon was surprised to find he was enjoying himself immensely. There was something freeing talking to this woman who was a total stranger and had no expectations of him at all.

'Is it cynical to observe the truth?' She pushed on. 'This distant relative is unfortunate-looking, with a lazy eye, yellowed teeth and rapidly thinning hair that he arranges in a way he hopes will hide the fact he hasn't much left. But you have been raised to appreciate no one can help how they look so you push aside all thoughts of their physical appearance.'

Simon pressed his lips together. Miss James had an amusing way of telling a story, and he urged her to continue. 'I am channelling those very thoughts,' he said.

'Good. Then he reaches out and with a sweaty palm lays a hand on your shoulder. A fleeting touch you could forgive, but the hand lingers far too long, and all the while his eyes do not move from your chest.'

'He is not sounding very enticing.'

'Then throughout the evening he makes his horrible opinions known on everything from how the poor should be punished for the awful situations they find themselves in to slavery to how it is God's plan for the lower levels of society to be decimated by illness that spreads more when people live in close conditions.'

'I am beginning to see why he is vile.'

'And he does all this whilst trying to squeeze your knee under the table.'

'Your parents are happy for you to marry him?'

Miss James sighed. 'Last year my sister…' She bit her lip again, drawing his gaze for a moment. 'I probably shouldn't tell you this.' Then she shrugged and continued. 'Yet our paths are never going to cross again.'

'What if I add in the extra layer of security by swearing I will never breathe a word of this to anyone.'

'You are a man of your word?'

'I never break an oath.'

'Last year my sister was caught up in a bit of a scandal. Rumours of late-night liaisons with a married gentleman. For a month she and I were forbidden to leave the house, and my parents thought we might even have to leave Bamburgh and move elsewhere. Thankfully a friend of my father's stepped in and proposed marriage to my sister to save her and the rest of our family from scandal.'

'Did it work?'

'Yes, although there are still a few people who cross the street to avoid my mother and me if we are out shopping. My sister is happy as mistress of her own home, living down in Devon, and she has a baby on the way. All things for a short while we thought she might never have.'

'This has pushed your parents to make an unwise match for you?'

'I think they are panicked. They are aware the taint of scandal can linger for a long time, and they keep reminding me I am already one and twenty. There are no local unmarried young men of the right social class so they decided they would arrange the only match that was assured.'

'Could you not refuse?'

Miss James laughed, but there was no bitterness in her tone, just pure amusement.

'We live in very different worlds, my Lord. I have no money of my own, no income, no way of supporting myself. I cannot even boast of a very good education so I doubt anyone would employ me as a governess. My value comes in marrying someone who can support me and any future children and remove that burden from my parents.'

'Vile Cecil is wealthy?'

'Moderately so. Enough to satisfy my parents. He is eager to be married and comes tomorrow to stay to discuss our engagement.'

'He has not asked you yet?'

'No, but that part is a mere formality.' She closed her eyes. 'So you see, this is my one last chance to dance at a ball with whoever I choose, to get a little tipsy with punch and to take ill-advised strolls along the terrace with mysterious gentlemen.'

'Then, we must ensure you have the best night of your life.'

Chapter Two

Alice felt a little giddy with recklessness. She should never have spoken of the things she had told Lord Westcroft, but it had been liberating to talk so freely. She could be confident that after tonight her path would never cross with the earl's again. In a few weeks she would be Mrs Cecil Billington, living a life of misery in some rural part of Suffolk where she knew no one except her odious husband.

'I think we need more punch,' Lord Westcroft said, bowing to her and disappearing inside before she could object. She had only drunk alcohol a few times before, small sips of wine with dinner, and she didn't know what was in the punch, but she was already feeling the wonderful warmth spreading out from her stomach around her body.

He returned with two more glasses and handed her one. As he walked back to her Alice was aware of all the curious stares they received from the other guests. No doubt everyone knew who Lord Westcroft was, and they would probably be wondering who he was spending all this time with. Alice tried to shrink into herself, feeling suddenly self-conscious.

'A toast, to one final night of freedom before you are condemned to a life with vile Cecil.'

Alice smiled, raising her glass and then putting it to her lips. She had never met an earl before, but she had not expected one to be like Lord Westcroft. He was surprisingly easy to talk to and had a laid-back manner that reminded her more of the young lads in the village than what she pictured an aristocrat would be like.

'How about you?' she said after she had drained half her glass. 'I've told you my deepest secrets. It is only fair I hear one of yours.'

For a moment she wondered if she had gone too far as his expression darkened, but after a second he placed his glass on the balustrade and leaned forward, looking out into the darkness of the garden.

'Shall I tell you something I have told no one else yet?' There was a sudden serious note in his voice.

Alice nodded, feeling her pulse quicken.

'I have never danced a waltz in the open air before.' He grinned at her and then held out his hand.

'I thought you were going to confess something serious,' she said, unable to stop herself from grinning at him in relief.

'You are keeping me waiting, Miss James. May I have this dance?'

'Everyone will stare at us.'

'That is true.'

'I am trying not to draw attention to myself.'

'It is far too late to be worried about that. Everyone is staring already.'

'How do you stand all the interest in you?'

'You grow accustomed to it.'

He held out his hand, and Alice took it despite the sensible part of her cautioning against it.

Inside, the first few notes of the waltz had started, and there were a dozen couples on the dance floor, twirling and stepping in time to the music.

She felt a thrill of pleasure as Lord Westcroft placed a hand in the small of her back and, exerting a gentle pressure, began to guide her into her first spin. He was an excellent dancer; he made it look effortless, and once Alice had got her confidence she was able to lift her eyes to meet his and just enjoy the dance knowing he would not let her slip.

For a few minutes she forgot there were other people at the ball: it was just her and Lord Westcroft, dancing under the stars. Every time they spun she felt her body sway a little closer to his, and once or twice his legs brushed hers. As the music swelled and then faded, she felt suddenly bereft and had to chide herself for the romantic thoughts that were trying to push to the fore in her mind.

'Thank you for the dance, Miss James,' Lord Westcroft said, bowing to her, his lips hovering over her hand.

She thought he might leave her then. They had spent well over half an hour together, dancing and talking and sipping punch in the moonlight, and it was not advisable for a gentleman to spend too much time with any one young lady or rumours would begin to circulate. The sensible thing for Lord Westcroft to do would be to bid her farewell and go dance with another young lady.

For a moment she saw him contemplate doing just that. He glanced over his shoulder, looking at the ballroom with an expression of trepidation. Then he turned back to her with a smile.

'Would you like to go for a stroll?'

'A stroll?'

'Only along the terrace and back. Perhaps a few dozen times. I find myself reluctant to let you go just yet, Miss James. I have this fear you will disappear as soon as I look away for an instant.'

'You wouldn't prefer to go and dance with someone else?'

'No,' he said simply.

'Then, I would enjoy a stroll very much.'

He offered her his arm, and she slipped her hand through and rested it in the crook of his elbow. They had only taken a few steps when they were cut off by a statuesque woman in a beautiful green and gold dress. Even with her mask on, Alice recognised Lady Salisbury. There was an expression of concerned curiosity on her face as she positioned herself directly in their path.

'Lord Westcroft, I hope you are enjoying the ball.'

'I am, thank you, Lady Salisbury.'

The viscountess turned to Alice, and Alice felt something shrivel inside her. There was coldness in the older woman's expression that hadn't been there when she had been looking at Lord Westcroft.

'I do not think we have been introduced, Miss…' Lady Salisbury said with a smile that did not reach her eyes.

Alice felt her mouth go instantly dry and her tongue stick to the roof.

'You must forgive me,' Lord Westcroft said before Alice could summon any words. 'I have a little confession to make.'

'Oh?' Lady Salisbury said, not taking her eyes off Alice.

'This is Miss James, a distant relative on my mother's side. She has been staying with my mother these past few weeks. When my mother heard I was attending your ball, she requested I ask you if Miss James could come as my guest, but I completely forgot. When Miss James appeared at my door in my mother's carriage tonight, I panicked and pretended you had agreed to her coming. I have to admit I hoped no one would notice and no word would get back to my mother about my oversight.'

Lady Salisbury looked from Lord Westcroft to Alice and back again for a moment and then broke out into a smile.

'Lord Westcroft, you should have just brought Miss James to me when you arrived. You know I can never deny you anything. He is charming, is he not, Miss James?'

'He is,' Alice agreed.

'I beg your forgiveness,' Lord Westcroft said and then leaned in closer to Lady Salisbury and spoke in a conspiratorial manner. 'And I beg you do not tell my mother of my error.'

'My lips are sealed, Lord Westcroft.'

'Now, Miss James, we cannot have the earl monopolising your time and attention at the ball tonight. I am sure there are many other gentlemen you wish to have the chance to dance with.'

'I have been selfish,' Lord Westcroft said, smiling indulgently at Alice as a distant relative might. 'I promise, once we have finished our stroll, to deliver Miss James to the ballroom where she can enjoy the attentions of all the gentlemen here tonight, clamouring to fill her dance-card.'

Lady Salisbury inclined her head and took her leave, glancing over her shoulder at them before she reentered the ballroom. Alice waited until she was sure the older woman was out of earshot to exhale loudly.

'I cannot breathe,' she said, trying to suck in large gasps of air.

'Be calm, Miss James. Lady Salisbury's suspicions are averted for now.'

'I thought she was going to rip my mask from my face and declare me an intruder, then command her footmen to escort me off her property.'

'I would not put it past her. She does not have the most forgiving of natures.'

'I need to leave,' Alice said desperately.

'That is the last thing you should do.'

She looked up at him, incredulous. He was remarkably calm, but she supposed if his lie was found out, it wouldn't really affect him. Lady Salisbury would forgive the earl, it would be Alice who would be thrown out in disgrace.

'Right now Lady Salisbury is watching you closely. If she sees you scurrying away she will know you were not meant to be here.'

'What do you suggest, then?'

'We stroll along the terrace as we had planned, and then you return to the ballroom and dance with a few different gentlemen before slipping away unnoticed.'

'I do not know if my nerves can stand it.'

He leaned in a little closer, his breath tickling her ear as he spoke. 'I'll be with you.'

* * *

Simon knew he was acting recklessly, but he could not find it in himself to care. No one knew who Miss James was or where she came from, so he did not have to worry as much as he normally would when spending time with a young lady. If he were honest, this evening was the first time he'd enjoyed himself quite so much in a long time, and it was because of Miss James.

In two weeks he would have left England, never to return, so for once he did not have to worry if he were upsetting anyone. There was no requirement for him to nod politely whilst an elderly acquaintance regaled him with a tiresome tale or an eager social climber thrust her daughter in his direction. Tonight he could do whatever he wanted safe in the knowledge that he would never see most of these people ever again. All he had to do was ensure he did not ruin Miss James in the process.

He watched her as they strolled along the terrace, reaching the end in less than a minute despite walking sedately. As they walked, some of the tension seeped from her shoulders, and before they turned back to head in the other direction she was smiling again.

'This is by far the most reckless thing I have ever done,' she said, leaning in so no one else could hear her words. 'I expect you do wild things all the time.'

'Once…' he said, almost wistfully. A few years ago his life had been charmed, although he hadn't been aware of it at the time. He'd lost his father when he was just twelve years old, and for a long time the grief had affected him, but five years ago things had been good. He had been surrounded by people who loved him—his mother, his older brother, his sister-in-law and his lovely nieces—and he'd had the freedom to do whatever he chose. As the second son, the title and the responsibility were never meant to be his. Robert was fair and loving and had ensured Simon had a home of his own and enough income to live a comfortable life. He'd relished his freedom then, the ability to go off at a moment's notice, to follow his desires on a whim.

They reached the end of the terrace again and turned, Simon glancing into the ballroom. Lady Salisbury was still watching them as she spoke to an elderly couple. Her eyes were narrowed slightly, and Simon realised she was still suspicious of his companion.

'Perhaps we should get you out of here,' he murmured, glancing at the steps that led to the garden.

'Surely Lady Salisbury would notice. I can feel her eyes on me.'

'You're right,' he said, feeling a little disappointed. There was something appealing about slipping into the darkened gardens in the company of Miss James. 'Let us go into the ballroom.'

'I feel so sick I might be sick over the shoes of whatever gentleman I am meant to dance with.'

'Don't do that,' he said with a smile. 'That is a sure way to get yourself noticed.'

He led her inside, his eyes dancing over the groups of people before resting on the person he was looking for.

'Forrester, good to see you,' he said, clapping a man of around his age on the back.

'Northumberland,' Forrester said with a grin. He leaned in closer, giving Miss James an appraising look. 'How do you manage to always end up with the most beautiful woman in the room on your arm?'

'Forrester, meet Miss James. Miss James, this is a good friend of mine from my schooldays, Mr Nicholas Forrester.'

Forrester bent over Alice's hand, giving her his most charming smile.

'We need a favour,' Simon said quickly. 'Will you dance the next dance with Miss James? Keep her away from Lady Salisbury. If our hostess asks who she is, tell her she's a distant relative of my mother's.'

'Is that the truth?'

'No.'

Forrester looked intrigued. 'You haven't smuggled one of your mistresses into this society affair, have you, Northumberland?'

Next to him he saw Miss James blush, and he quickly shook his head. 'No, Miss James is completely respectable. Will you dance with her as a favour?'

'No favour needed. Would you do me the honour, Miss James?'

She inclined her head, and Simon watched as Forrester lead her to the dance floor. They had a few minutes before the next dance was called, and he realised he felt a spark of jealousy as Forrester bent his head close to Miss James's to discuss something over the hum of conversation in the room.

He should move on, find some débutante to talk to, so if Lady Salisbury glanced in his direction she would see nothing suspicious, only an unmarried gentleman talking to a woman with a sizeable dowry. Simon cast his eyes around the room, but after a few seconds he found he was drawn back to where Miss James stood with Forrester. They were both smiling now, and he felt a prickle of unease. He hoped she hadn't told Forrester of her true identity.

With his eyes locked on the couple, he watched as they took their places for a quadrille. Miss James danced well for someone who had only been to a few dances at the local Assembly Rooms. Her steps were graceful, and her body swayed in time to the music. His eyes glided over her body, taking in the curve of her hips and her slender, pinched-in waist. For the first time in a long time he felt a surge of desire.

Shaking his head ruefully he forced himself to focus on something else. Desire had no place in his life now, but he would not punish himself for merely appreciating a beautiful woman.

'You're prowling,' Maria said as she approached, her voice low and filled with mirth.

'Prowling? You make me sound like an animal.'

'You *look* like an animal. Perhaps a wolf or a grumpy bear.'

'Just what every man wishes to be compared to,' he murmured.

'If you do not wish to be called a grumpy bear, perhaps do not frown so. Balls are meant to be fun.'

He plastered an exaggerated smile on his face and watched as Maria recoiled.

'For the love of everything that is holy, please stop,' she said. 'How old are you?'

'Thirty-two.'

'Then, why must you act as if you were five?'

'Only for you, my dearest sister.'

Maria was only a few years older than him. She had married his older brother, Robert, when she was nineteen and Robert twenty-three. Simon had been thirteen at the time and reeling from his father's sudden death. Maria had seen a boy struggling with the world and given him the kindness that no one else in his family could at that moment, grieving as they all were, and Simon would never forget it. Over the years their relationship had grown and changed with each new stage of life, but now he was blessed with a sister-in-law who he loved as if she were his own flesh and blood.

'She is pretty,' Maria said, motioning to where Miss James twirled on the dance floor.

'Mmm…' Simon responded. Maria didn't know of his plans to leave England yet. He hadn't told her of the passage he had booked to Europe or his expectation he would never be back. His sister-in-law had suffered so much over the last few years, he knew his departure would devastate her. He would tell her: he wasn't so much of a brute as to leave without saying goodbye, but he didn't want there to be too much time between his revelation and his departure. If anyone could get him to change his mind, it would be Maria.

'Do you know her from somewhere?'

'No,' Simon said, and then glanced over his shoulder. 'But if Lady Salisbury asks, she's a distant relative of my mother's.'

Maria raised an eyebrow. 'What are you doing, Simon?' Then her face lit up with pure joy. 'Are you courting her?'

'Good Lord, no,' he said, pulling Maria to one side, looking round to check no one else had heard her words. He was considered a highly eligible bachelor, with his title, wealth and single status despite being into his thirties. *Everyone* was waiting for him to declare he was finally ready to start looking for a wife. He didn't need any flames being added to that fire.

'Then, who is she?'

'A pleasant young woman I met about an hour ago.'

'Why are you watching her so closely?'

'I'm not,' he said, realising his eyes were on her again. With an effort he looked away and focussed on his sister-in-law.

'Whatever you are doing, be careful,' Maria cautioned him. She flitted between the role of a protective older sister and an excitable friend. There were many people he was going to miss when he left, and Maria was close to the top of that list.

The music swelled and the dance finished, and Simon watched as Forrester bowed to Miss James. They lingered for a moment, talking quietly, before Forrester escorted Miss James to the edge of the dance floor.

'Excuse me,' Simon said, hoping Maria did not follow him, moving quickly to scoop Miss James up before anyone else could. Lady Salisbury was on the other side of the room now and seemed to momentarily have lost interest in the young woman. It would be a good opportunity to sneak Miss James back out the way she had come.

'Thank you for the dance, Miss James,' Forrester said as Simon approached. 'I think Northumberland would run me through with a sword if I asked you to dance again, but I do hope you have an enjoyable evening.'

Once Forrester had left, Simon leaned in as close as he dared and said quietly, 'Lady Salisbury is otherwise occupied. I wonder if it would be best to sneak you out of here now.'

Chapter Three

With her heart hammering in her chest Alice tried to act nonchalant as she followed Lord Westcroft from the ballroom. She looked all around for Lydia but could not see her anywhere and wondered if Lady Salisbury had recognised her as an interloper as well. It was more likely Lydia had realised Lady Salisbury was watching her and slipped away herself. Her friend was highly excitable but astute and observant. Hopefully she was halfway back to the village by now.

'We stand here, pretending to talk, until no one is looking, then we quickly walk down the steps into the darkness of the garden.'

'What if someone sees us?'

'They won't.'

'Would it be safer for me to go by myself?'

She saw him grimace and then shake his head. 'We do not know if anyone is roaming the gardens. There could be all sorts of dangers out there.'

'You make it sound as though wild animals prowl through the flower beds.'

'The truth is much more dangerous. There are un-scrupulous people in this world.'

Before Alice could protest any further, he grabbed her by the hand and pulled her down the steps into the shadows of one of the alcoves set below the terrace. They were completely hidden here, out of view from anyone on the terrace above or the ballroom beyond. Someone would have to come all the way down the stairs for them to be seen.

'We'll wait here for a moment and then make a run for it across the lawn,' Lord Westcroft said. His expression was serious, but Alice had a suspicion that he was enjoying himself. They stood quietly for a few minutes, Alice's hand tucked into Lord Westcroft's, and then he nodded to her, and together they set off across the lawn. All the time they were running, Alice felt exposed and was certain there would be a shout from the terrace, perhaps the pattering of feet as people descended the steps into the garden to identify them. Only once they were secreted behind a hedge did she allow herself to breathe normally.

She glanced back towards the house and was relieved to see no one was paying any particular attention to the garden. Hopefully they had made it across unnoticed. Lord Westcroft was also looking back, but after a moment his eyes lowered to meet hers.

Alice felt a spark of attraction between them. She knew much of it was from the excitement of the last few minutes, but she had the irrepressible urge to reach up and trail her fingers over Lord Westcroft's face. She was horrified to find her hand halfway up to his cheek and felt a wave of mortification as he caught it in his own.

'We should get you home, Miss James,' he murmured, holding onto her hand and making no move to leave.

She nodded, her eyes fixed on his.

Alice was never normally reckless. Never before to-night had she sneaked into anyplace she shouldn't be. She obeyed her parents' rules and conducted herself in a manner that was expected of an unmarried young woman. Yet she didn't pull away. She didn't turn her head or break eye contact.

Despite the worry of the last half an hour it had been a magical evening. For a few hours she had been able to pretend she was someone else, swept away in the glamour and opulence of the masquerade ball. For a time she had been able to forget the impending engagement she was about to be pushed into and dance and laugh as if she were free to do whatever she pleased.

Lord Westcroft's thumb caressed the back of her hand, and then before she could stop herself, she pushed up on her tiptoes and kissed him. It was a momentary brush of her lips against his, but as they came together something primal tightened deep inside her, and she realised she wanted so much more.

'Miss James,' he murmured as she pulled away, desire burning bright in his eyes. She thought he might reprimand her. All evening he had been a perfect gentleman, despite the attraction that crackled between them. For a long moment he did nothing, his body so close she could feel the heat of him, and then he gripped her around the waist and kissed her again.

This kiss was deep and passionate and made Alice forget where she was. His lips were soft against hers, and she could taste the sweetness of the punch they had both had. His scent was something entirely different, and she had to fight the urge to bury herself in his neck.

Alice felt her body sink into his, and in that moment all she could think about were his lips on hers. There were no thoughts of consequences, no thoughts of being sensible or respectable. It was just Lord Westcroft and his kiss.

They both stiffened and pulled apart at exactly the same moment. Somewhere to her left, coming from the direction of the house, was a rustling noise. For an instant Alice wondered if it could be an animal, and then the sound came again and she knew for certain it was another person. Whether it was a couple who had slipped into the gardens for some privacy, or one of the servants patrolling to ensure no one was sneaking in after Lady Salisbury's suspicions had been roused, it didn't matter. Someone else was there in the gardens, and if they were caught there would be a horrific scandal.

Alice felt a cold shudder run through her. It would be a repeat of what had happened with her sister, only worse. At least Margaret had a gentleman who had been happy to marry her and save her from the scandal. She doubted even vile Cecil would take her if she got caught kissing the earl in the garden whilst attending a party she had not been invited to.

'I have to go,' she said, pulling away sharply.

'Wait,' Lord Westcroft whispered, catching her hand. 'It might not be safe.'

'I have to go,' she repeated.

This time she wrenched her hand from his and set off at a run across the gardens. She had an advantage, following the route she had crept through with Lydia only a few hours earlier. She weaved around flower beds, squeezed through hedges and pushed herself over fences.

At first she fancied she heard footsteps behind her and thought Lord Westcroft was following her, but somewhere after she had squeezed through the second hedge she lost him.

Only once she was on the road that led back to the village did she slow, her chest heaving, to catch her breath. She desperately hoped Lydia had found her way home already and wasn't trapped somewhere by Lady Salisbury and her suspicions.

Despite the fear of being found out and the frantic dash back through the gardens, Alice could not find it in herself to regret the evening. She had been more reckless than she ever had before, or ever would be again, but for a few hours she had felt alive.

Chapter Four

Simon groaned as he rested his head in his hands, leaning forward onto the desk. He rubbed his temples, trying to alleviate the pounding. Headaches were part of his daily life now, horrible, pulsating episodes of pain that stopped him whatever he was doing and forced him to seek out the relief of a darkened room. For the last year he had been unable to deny that they were happening more frequently and getting worse.

Today however, his headache was a little different. It was the heavy fog caused by drinking too much alcohol, and it was completely self-inflicted.

There was a knock on the door, and he quickly straightened as his butler entered.

'The dowager countess is here, my Lord.'

'Show her in,' he said, hoping he didn't look too terrible.

Maria breezed in, stopping to regard him and shake her head like a fussy mother hen. 'You look terrible, Simon.'

'You look lovely.'

She tutted at his glib reply and sank down into a chair

across from him. 'I have never seen you drink as much as you did last night.'

After Miss James had fled through the gardens, he had followed her, only to lose her a few minutes later. For someone running in highly impractical satin shoes, she had moved fast. He was unsure if they had been spotted and had returned to the ball half expecting someone to come up and make some lewd remarks. As the evening had worn on without anyone saying anything, his relief had led him to the card room, and he had spent far too long playing cards and drinking whisky, trying to forget how good it had been to lose himself for a few minutes in Miss James's kiss.

'We have something very serious to discuss, Simon,' Maria said, her expression grave. For a moment he wondered if she had worked out he was suffering from the headaches. Maria was astute, and if anyone was going to uncover his secret it would be his sister-in-law. 'Last night, in the gardens, someone saw you.'

It took a moment for the words to sink in, and he cleared his throat.

'Who saw what?'

'I had a visit this morning from Miss Elizabeth Cheevers and her mother. It was unannounced and horribly awkward. It would seem they were in the village to shop for some material for a new dress, and when they stopped at the haberdasher's they overheard something disturbing.'

Simon sat a little straighter, his stomach sinking.

'Go on.'

'You were seen in the garden last night, kissing a young woman. By the description, it sounds like Miss

James, but they did not have a name to attach to the rumours as yet.'

Simon felt the world tilt and judder around him for a second, and he had to grip the arms of his chair to steady himself.

'This is bad, Simon,' Maria said, biting her lip. 'It is the talk of the village already, which means by tomorrow the whole county will likely know.'

'They will not know who Miss James is. She kept her mask on the whole time.'

'There are people out there who will make it their whole purpose in life to identify the young woman you were seen kissing. They will think it their moral duty.'

Simon stood and paced to the door and back, trying to order his thoughts. It would be easier if his head weren't pounding so much. For him the consequences were minimal. At worst he would get some snide remarks and a few people avoiding him when he went out and about, but he was an earl and there was only a limited number of people who would dare be rude to him. Added to that, with his plans to leave England in a few weeks, it would hardly affect him.

Miss James was another matter entirely. There was a small hope that she would not be identified. As she was not an invited guest, she would not be the first person to be suspected, but with her distinctive red hair and pretty blue eyes he doubted she would stay hidden for long. He cursed his own stupidity of giving Lady Salisbury her real name, but last night in the moment of their hostess's questioning he had not thought her name would matter.

He closed his eyes. This was the last thing he needed

right now. His plans to leave England could not be disrupted.

'Do not be so selfish,' he muttered to himself, then turned to Maria. 'Please excuse me. I have to try to put this right.'

'You're going to see her?'

'I have to.'

'People will be watching what you do and where you go.'

'I can be discreet.'

'I do not doubt it, but please be careful. I did not speak to Miss James for long, but she seemed a sweet young woman.'

Simon inclined his head and then strode from the room. There was no time to waste. He needed to get to Miss James before the gossip started circling.

Alice sat demurely, her hands folded in her lap and a serene expression fixed on her face, all the while trying not to burst into tears. Across the room her mother sat beaming at her and their new guest. Cecil Billington had been placed beside her on the sofa and had gradually inched closer until his knees were almost touching hers.

'I think you would like Ensley, Miss James,' Cecil said, smiling at her with his mouth full of crooked, yellow teeth. He reached out and boldly stroked the back of her hand as he spoke, and Alice had to use all her self-control to stop herself from pulling away abruptly.

'It is a pleasant village?'

'On the whole, yes. There are plenty of like-minded people to socialise with and a few decent shops. There are more poor people than I would like, but I am working with the other local landlords to raise the rents so we only get a certain class of people in the village. You cannot eliminate the lower classes entirely—we need somewhere for our servants and the people who provide the essential services for the village to live—but I have proposed a system to limit the numbers.'

'Where will the people go who do not make the cut?' Alice asked coldly.

Cecil shrugged. 'That is not my concern. You understand the idea is to make the village a more agreeable place. A place where children can skip freely down the streets and women can walk without fear in the evenings.'

'I thought you said it was a pleasant place already,' Alice said and tried to ignore the warning look she received from her mother.

'Let us not talk of Ensley,' Cecil said, shifting ever closer. 'I am very much looking forward to my stay here, Miss James. I hope you will allow me to accompany you on your daily business.'

'Alice would like that very much,' Mrs James said quickly.

Alice smiled sweetly. 'Today I am going to take a basket of food to Mrs Willow and her children. Mr Willow died last year of consumption, and I understand two of the children have been unwell.'

Alice's mother inhaled loudly and as Alice glanced over gave her a stern look. Cecil looked appalled as she had known he would and shifted uncomfortably.

'Surely you cannot mean to visit a family where there is illness, Miss James? You have to think of yourself.'

'I promised Mrs Willow I would go. She struggles with six children now she is all by herself.'

Cecil curled his lip and flexed his fingers where they rested on her hand.

'Even in the summer months we must be vigilant against disease,' he said.

'Perhaps you could postpone the visit for a few days, Alice,' Mrs James said firmly. 'I am sure Mr Billington would appreciate your time being spent to show him a little of the village and the surrounding area. It is a glorious day. You might even take a stroll on the beach.'

'A promise is a promise, Mother,' Alice said quickly. 'I am sure Mr Billington would not want me to brush off my commitments so readily. It is not an attractive quality in a woman to be unreliable.'

She was saved from further argument by the door opening and their maid slipping into the room. They were not a grand household. Her father's income could only provide enough for one maid and a young lad who helped both inside the house and in the garden. Milly helped Alice's mother in the kitchen and did some of the housework duties around the house, but Alice was expected to do her fair share. All of which had increased significantly since her sister had left home.

'There is a gentleman to see Miss James,' Milly said, turning over a small card in her fingers. She looked in awe of the little piece of embossed card.

'A gentleman?' Mrs James said, standing and casting an apologetic look at Cecil.

'Yes, ma'am,' Milly lowered her voice. 'He says he's the Earl of Northumberland.'

Mrs James's eyes widened, and she took a step forward before turning to Alice.

'Alice James, if this is one of your friends being silly, I will not be impressed.'

In any other circumstance Alice would have had to suppress a smile. It *was* the sort of thing Lydia would do, press an unsuspecting male friend or relative into giving Milly a card with a false name upon it. However, today Alice knew it was no trick.

She felt her mouth go dry and her pulse quicken. There was no good reason for him to be here. Last night had been magical, but Alice was well aware it had been an interlude in her otherwise normal life, nothing more. Lord Westcroft had no place in her small drawing room in their modest home in Bamburgh, just as she had no place in the lofty halls of his grand country house.

'Shall I show him in?' Milly asked, her hand hovering on the door-handle.

'Yes, you had better,' Mrs James said, glancing at Alice again. 'Do you know him?'

Before Alice could answer the door opened again, and Lord Westcroft stepped into the room. He looked out of place in the drab drawing room, and Alice suddenly felt self-conscious. In the cold light of day he would see her dress was made of inferior material, her hands dry and reddened by the manual labour she had to undertake. Normally these things did not bother her, but in front of him she felt a fraud, an imposter. Last night she had soared with all the wealthy ladies, the candlelight allowing her to pass as one of them. It would be painfully clear today she did not fit with the women he was accustomed to.

As he entered the room Alice thought back to the perfect kiss they had shared in the garden before she had fled through the night. It had been magical, everything a young woman could dream of for her first kiss. She found her eyes flicking to his lips now and had to force herself to look away, to focus on the floor as she bobbed into an unsteady little curtsy.

'It is an honour to have you in our home, my Lord,' Mrs James said, bustling over and pausing in front of the earl.

'I am sorry to call unannounced. I hope you can forgive me for dropping in like this.'

'You know an earl?' Cecil muttered out of the corner of his mouth, spittle gathering in the corners in a little frothy bubble.

'A little,' Alice said warily. Lord Westcroft had seemed a sensible man last night and had been aware of the damage that could be done to her reputation by the wrong association. She knew he would not be here if it weren't important. She thought of the rustle in the bushes the night before as they had shared their kiss, the feeling that someone had spotted them, that eyes were watching them, and she shuddered.

'Miss James,' Lord Westcroft said, turning to her with a dazzling smile, 'it is delightful to see you again.'

'And you, my Lord,' Alice said, trying to read his expression.

'And this must be your dear cousin you were telling me about,' Lord Westcroft said, directing his gaze onto Cecil. Alice caught the mischief in the earl's eye and pressed her lips together giving a miniscule shake of her head.

'Billington, Cecil Billington, at your service, my Lord,' Cecil said, stretching out a hand to shake Lord Westcroft's.

'Forgive me, my Lord. I was not aware you were acquainted with my daughter.'

'Our acquaintance has not been a lengthy one,' Lord Westcroft said, allowing Mrs James to usher him into the room. The room was not large, and alongside a low table there was only the armchair Mrs James had been sitting in and the long sofa where Alice and Cecil were. Lord Westcroft seemed unperturbed and took a place next to Alice on the other side.

As they sat his leg brushed hers, and she glanced up at him. For a moment it seemed like they were the only two people in the room; everyone else had faded into the background. Then Cecil cleared his throat, and Alice was pulled right back to reality, sandwiched between the man who could ruin her future and the man she desperately wished she did not have to spend a lifetime tied to.

For one heady moment she wondered if Lord Westcroft had decided to come and rescue her, to declare himself in love after their one evening spent together. Then she looked at his serious expression and knew that wasn't the case.

'Miss James and I met through the course of some of her charitable works,' Lord Westcroft said smoothly. Alice nodded a little too eagerly at the lie and had to tell herself to calm down. Her mother would think it suspicious she had not mentioned meeting a man of his status, although she was hardly going to contradict the earl to his face.

Alice had told Lord Westcroft the evening before of her scheme to pair some of the wealthier families in the village with some of the poorer ones, to provide support over the harsher winters, little parcels of firewood or baskets of food. By joining families one on one, she hoped the wealthier ones would start to feel a little responsibility to their less fortunate counterparts. It would make it harder to distance themselves from the tribulations and struggles of the people they could help.

'I am very keen to get involved with your endeavours, Miss James. I wondered if you might be able to spare me some time to discuss things this morning.'

Alice searched his face, trying to work out what had prompted this visit, but his expression was impassive, a bland smile that was meant to alleviate the concerns of the other people in the room.

'Miss James and I were planning on going for a walk over the dunes,' Cecil said, leaning forward to insert himself into the conversation. 'I understand Miss James's friend is going to make herself available to chaperon.'

'Excellent,' Lord Westcroft said. 'I apologise, Mr Billington, for interrupting your plans like this, but I will not forget your generosity in giving up your time with Miss James for me.'

Cecil opened his mouth and closed it again a few times. It was clear he had meant to accompany Lord Westcroft and Alice on the walk, inserting himself into whatever business they were about to discuss, but Lord Westcroft had quickly outmanoeuvred him.

'Perhaps we should go now, Miss James. I have an appointment this afternoon I wish to keep.'

'Lydia is planning on meeting you?' Mrs James said quickly. Lord Westcroft might be an earl, but the rules of polite society still applied. Even though no one would ever think he could be interested in the likes of Alice, they still had to safeguard her reputation.

'Yes, Mama. She is going to meet us on the beach in twenty minutes.'

'Wonderful,' Lord Westcroft said, rising to his feet. 'It was a pleasure to meet you, Mrs James, and you, Mr Billington.' He bowed to the older woman and shook Cecil's outstretched hand, surreptitiously wiping his hand on his jacket after doing so. Then before anyone could think of any objections, he offered Alice his arm, and quickly they left the room together.

'Let me get my bonnet,' Alice said, running upstairs to fetch it and tie it securely under her chin. It was a glorious day out, but the wind was strong, whipping off the sea with a ferocity that was not common for this time of year. Her skin was so pale it only took a few minutes in the sunlight to turn pink and then burn, but with the wind it was even worse, and she didn't doubt she would have red cheeks later despite her precautions.

They left the house quickly, and Alice was pleased to find they were, so far, unobserved. Her home was on the outskirts of Bamburgh village, at the bottom past the castle that stood proud on the rocky hill. It meant the beach was in easy reach, and they would not have to walk along the high street to get there.

For a few minutes they walked in silence, both looking around all the time to see if they were being watched. Only when they got to the edge of the dunes did Alice feel herself relax.

Waiting as she had promised was Lydia, her eyes alight with intrigue and excitement. As she saw Alice approach on Lord Westcroft's arm she frowned, standing a little straighter.

'This cannot be vile Cecil,' Lydia said quietly as they

approached, clapping her hands over her mouth as soon as the words were out in a bid to claw them back in. Her eyes narrowed, and she shook her head. 'I recognise you.' Five seconds passed and then ten, and then realisation dawned on her.

'Lydia, please,' Alice said quickly. 'Do not make a fuss.'

'This is Lord Westcroft, Earl of Northumberland,' she said, jabbing a finger in his direction. 'The most eligible bachelor in all of England. Last seen at Lady Salisbury's ball last night with a mystery woman in blue.' Lydia turned to her. 'I saw you dancing with him. Although, I didn't know who he was at the time. You're the mystery woman people are talking about.'

Alice felt her heart sink. She had hoped Lord Westcroft was here for some other reason, but deep down she supposed she had known that it was as a consequence of their actions the night before.

'Everyone is saying he was spotted kissing some unknown guest at Lady Salisbury's ball in the gardens.'

Lord Westcroft groaned.

'We were seen?' Alice asked, turning to him.

'It would appear so. I understand gossip and speculation is rampaging through the county.'

Alice felt the world around her tilt, and she clutched a little tighter at Lord Westcroft's arm.

'That is why I thought it imperative to come this morning.'

'Do people know it was me?'

'Not yet,' Lord Westcroft said, stopping and waiting until Alice looked up at him, 'but I think it is inevitable.'

Chapter Five

Alice felt her legs almost give way underneath her, and she was glad of Lord Westcroft's arm supporting her own.

'Perhaps we could take a walk along the beach, Miss James,' Lord Westcroft said, his voice calm. 'We have much to talk about.'

'Everyone will know,' Alice said, shaking her head. She felt sick and hot and as if her whole life were about to implode around her.

'Please, Miss James. I implore you to remain calm,' Lord Westcroft said, his voice silky smooth, and Alice felt some of the panic recede. Perhaps he had a plan, some way of diverting suspicion from her.

In front of her Lydia stood, eyes wide, hardly able to believe what was happening.

'You should do what Lord Westcroft asks, Alice,' Lydia said, motioning for them to go ahead of her across the sand dunes. 'I am sure you have much to discuss.'

Thankfully the wind had kept most people away from the beach, and there were only a few couples in the far distance strolling along the damp sand. Alice picked a path through the dune and onto the beach itself, having to hitch up her skirt as she traversed the soft sand. The climb up the dunes was strenuous even though they were not high along this part of the coast, but the sand was powdery soft, and if you didn't put your feet in exactly the right place you slipped down again. Once at the top she paused for a second to catch her breath and check Lord Westcroft was following her, thinking he might find the unfamiliar terrain difficult, but he was directly behind her, traversing the dunes like a steady-footed mountain goat.

She slipped and slid down the other side, stopping at the bottom to wait for Lord Westcroft and Lydia.

'I'll walk behind,' Lydia said, giving Alice's arm a reassuring squeeze. 'Close enough to count as a chaperon but far enough to give you some privacy.'

'Thank you,' Alice said. She knew how lucky she was to have Lydia as a friend. Not only was the young woman full of spirit and the joys of life, she was loyal and kind too. One of her greatest fears about leaving Bamburgh and starting her life anew, apart from the horror of being married to vile Cousin Cecil, was leaving Lydia behind. She desperately wanted to know how Lydia had fared at the ball the evening before but pushed her questions to the back of her mind. There would be plenty of time for her to catch up with her friend later.

'Come, Miss James. Our time together is short, and we have much to discuss.'

Lord Westcroft led her across the sand. They walked just below the high-tide mark, the sand still damp under their feet. The beach was beautifully clean, the sea clear, with hardly any seaweed deposited on the sand. Alice adjusted her bonnet as they walked, pulling it down a little lower to protect her from the sun.

'My sister-in-law came to see me earlier this morning,' Lord Westcroft said, wasting no time now they were alone. 'She tells me last night we were seen in the garden.' He paused and glanced at her before returning his gaze to the horizon. 'Kissing.'

'Someone actually saw us kiss?' Alice asked, horrified. It would have been ruinous to be merely seen sneaking off into the gardens unchaperoned with the earl, but if someone had seen them kiss, it was impossible to argue there was some innocent explanation for their presence in the garden.

'They did,' Lord Westcroft said. He was looking straight ahead, his posture stiff, and Alice realised he must have come straight to seek her out after he had been informed they had been seen. She felt a swell of gratitude for this man who had shown her kindness the night before and for a short while had made her dream of something other than the future that she was destined for. He could have brushed away the gossip; it would hardly have touched him. A few people might whisper behind their hands when they saw him, but being subject to such gossip would hardly affect his life at all. There were no consequences for men of his social status, not like there were for women of hers. Yet he had still hurried to her, seeking to reach her before the gossips identified her as the mystery woman and ruined her life.

'There is a chance no one will find out who you are,' Lord Westcroft said, glancing at her and grimacing. 'Although, you do have quite distinctive hair. I doubt there is anyone else in all of Northumberland with hair the same shade as yours. Now I think of it I am sure it is why Lady Salisbury was so suspicious at the ball.'

'So the likelihood I remain unidentified is small,' Alice said quietly. She could see her whole life crashing down around her. The devastation it would cause her parents, the end of her life as she knew it. Even Cousin Cecil would declare her too damaged for marriage. She wondered if her sister might take her in: surely the scandal wouldn't reach all the way to Devon. It would be a horrible existence, though, always wondering if someone might know someone who had told them of her infamy.

'Yes. I think you have to prepare yourself for the very real possibility that you will be identified. Of course, there is no proof. You could decide to bluster the whole affair out, especially if you can get your parents on your side. If they swear you did not leave home last night, then I am sure no one will come out and call them liars directly.'

Alice considered the suggestion. 'You mean let people gossip and speculate but deny everything and hope with time things settle down.'

'It might work, and it would mean you could continue your normal life.' He stopped walking for a moment, turning to her and running a hand through his hair. 'I haven't even said I'm sorry, Miss James,' he said and gave her a sad smile. 'I am, from the bottom of my heart. I'm sorry. I shouldn't have kissed you. I have been playing society's game for long enough. I should have been more careful.' He shook his head. 'I pride myself on being a practical person, yet I let myself get carried away.'

'It was not all your fault,' Alice said. 'I kissed you first.'

'I think we were both caught up in the magic of the moment,' he said, his eyes flicking to her lips for a fraction of a second. Alice felt a bolt of anticipation run through her, and she wondered if he felt it too, for he turned away abruptly, offering her his arm again.

For a minute neither of them spoke, and Alice got the sense Lord Westcroft was building up to something. She looked out to sea, trying to imagine her life with the shadow of this kiss hanging over it. She realised, despite what was to come, she couldn't bring herself to regret the evening entirely. She wished she had been more careful, that no one had seen their moment of intimacy in the garden, but she could not wish she had never gone. It had been the first time she had abandoned caution and allowed herself to enjoy the moment, and it had been wonderful from start to finish.

'Vile Cecil arrived as planned I see,' Lord Westcroft said, surprising Alice with his change of direction.

'Yes. I understand he stayed over in Belford last night so he could ride the last few miles this morning. I thought I might have a few more hours before he descended upon us, but it was not to be.'

'Has he proposed yet?'

Alice shook her head. 'No.' She bit her lip and felt her heart sink. 'You think I should press him to before any of the rumours reach him.'

'No,' Lord Westcroft said quickly. 'I would not wish that on anyone, not unless that is what you want.' He paused and then looked at her intently again. 'I just want you to realise what options you have. All is not lost. There is the possibility to live a normal life.'

Alice felt a sudden spark of anger. It felt as though he

were doing his very best to come up with a solution that did not involve him. If he were any sort of gentleman, he would at least mention the idea of marrying her. Alice was not so naïve to think an earl would ever actually end up with a young woman like her, but it would be courteous to at least pretend he would consider it.

She was about to say something to that effect when he stopped walking and waited for her to turn to face him.

'There is another possibility, Miss James,' he said quietly, 'but I need you to really listen as I tell you what I can offer you and what I cannot.'

Alice felt her pulse quicken, and she suddenly wished there was somewhere to sit down, but the only place was the damp sand, and she didn't want to have to explain a wet, sandy dress to her mother.

'In two weeks I leave England,' he said, his expression completely serious with a hint of sadness. 'I plan to travel to the Continent and find somewhere quiet to make my home for the next few months. I have been preparing for this trip for a long time, and I cannot postpone it. There are factors outside my control to consider.'

Alice remained silent, waiting for him to tell her more. It was clear he was not suggesting she accompany him.

'When I leave the country, I do not envisage ever coming back,' he said slowly, his words quiet but clear, and he regarded her intently as if needing to see she understood the gravity of what he was saying. 'Are you aware of my family's history at all?'

She shook her head.

'I was never meant to be earl. My father died when he should still have had a good number of years of life left. He was youthful and healthy, yet one day he just dropped down dead.' Lord Westcroft looked away for a moment, and Alice saw the glint of tears in his eyes. 'For the six months before he died he suffered from debilitating headaches, terrible daily pains that worsened week by week. Then one day he called out in pain, his face a picture of agony, and a few seconds later he collapsed on the floor, dead.'

Alice closed her eyes for a second, wanting to reach out and take Lord Westcroft's hand. He looked devastated, and she realised he must have witnessed his father's death.

'My brother, Robert, became the earl. He was ten years older than me, and for a while he looked out for me like a father. You met my sister-in-law last night. They married just after the mourning period for my father was complete and had three beautiful daughters. There was no reason to think they wouldn't have more children, that they wouldn't have a son who would inherit. I settled into my role as younger brother to the earl.'

Behind them Lydia had stopped too, just out of earshot, and Alice was pleased to see the beach remained almost empty. Horrible as his revelations so far had been, she felt like Lord Westcroft had worse to tell her.

'Then five years ago Robert started to get headaches. Every day he would wake up, and they would be worse than the last.'

Alice's hand went to her mouth. She knew Lord Westcroft's brother was dead, and she could now see where this story was headed. It was terrible.

'One day he dropped dead. He had been out for a ride with his wife and had just dismounted and then collapsed with no warning. The doctor said he was dead before he hit the ground.'

Reaching out Alice laid a hand on Lord Westcroft's arm. To lose one close relative in such a way was horrific, but two would be completely devastating.

He looked at her with haunted eyes and then spoke ever so quietly. 'A year ago I began experiencing headaches. Mild at first, and not every day, but over the last six months they have built in intensity. Every day they build and build until I am forced to lie down in a darkened room.'

'You think…' She couldn't bring herself to say the words.

'I have consulted doctors. They tell me there is nothing to be done and no way of telling when I might be struck down.'

Alice shook her head, unable to comprehend what living with such knowledge would do to you. Every moment he must live in fear of it being his last.

'I am sorry, my Lord. That is no way to live,' Alice said quietly.

'I have made my peace with it, but I have decided I do not want someone I love to witness my death. My mother has suffered enough, my sister-in-law too,' he said grimacing. 'And if I were to die in front of one of my nieces…' He shook his head. 'It is an intolerable thought.'

'This is why you are leaving the country?'

'Yes. I am going to find somewhere peaceful to rent a house, employ someone to cook and clean, pay them well for their services and inform them one day they might walk in to find me dead on the floor.'

Alice shook her head. 'Surely it would be better to

be amongst the people that love you, to spend however long you have with your family.'

Lord Westcroft spoke softly, but there was a steely determination in his voice that Alice realised was born from adversity. 'Every night when I go to sleep, when my thoughts are drifting and I no longer have conscious control of them, I see my father in the moment of his death. I relive the feelings of grief and devastation and shock over and over. I will not inflict that on anyone I love.'

He fell silent, and Alice pressed her lips together. He had lived with this burden for years and had had to face the question of his own mortality for a long time as well. It was not for her to question everything he had been through and the decisions he was making now as a consequence.

'I am sorry for everything you have been through,' Alice said, waiting until he looked at her and then holding his eye. 'It is more than any person should have to bear.'

'I have accepted this as my lot in life. I have had more than thirty years of living in comfort with a family who love me and a very privileged position in society. There are many who have much less than me.' He reached out and took her hand. It was an intimate gesture as Alice felt her heart quicken in her chest. 'I do not normally burden people with the whole story, but I think it is important for you to understand it all, to know exactly what it is I can offer you and what I cannot.'

The wind whipped around them as they stood together on the beach, blowing Alice's skirt against Lord Westcroft's legs, but he hardly seemed to notice.

'We find ourselves chased by scandal, Miss James,

and I think it inevitable your name will be associated with the kiss we shared, even if no one can prove it was you in that garden. I can offer you marriage, a protection of sorts, but it will not be the sort of marriage you expected for yourself.' He paused, checking she was following his words. 'If it is what you choose, I will marry you. It will save you from scandal, and once you become countess no one will care how we were a little careless. You will have my name and title as protection.'

Alice felt her head swim. Even from their short acquaintance she had known Lord Westcroft was an honourable man, but she had not expected this offer from him.

'I would obtain a special licence, and we would marry within the next few weeks. Then I would continue with my plan to leave the country.'

Alice's eyes flicked up to meet his, and she realised the importance of what he was saying and why he had told her exactly what had happened to his father and brother.

'You would be free to use whichever of my houses you wished, and I would ensure there was a good amount of money available for you. You would have a comfortable life, Miss James, but it would be a life spent on your own, at least at first.'

She opened her mouth to speak, but he pushed on quickly.

'Hear the last of my proposition,' he urged her. 'After we are married, you will not see me again. We will not consummate our union, and you will never bear me children. You will live as my wife in name until I die, and then you will be my widow.'

Alice took a step back, unable to take it all in. It was a generous proposition in so many ways, but she wasn't so naïve to think it the perfect solution to her problems. She would become a countess, an elevation in social status most women could only dream of, but Lord Westcroft had made it clear it would not be a normal marriage where their union would be celebrated. Alice tried to imagine her life if she did decide to marry Lord Westcroft. She would be mistress of her own home, finally in control of her own life, but it would be a lonely existence.

'There are some terms that I would ask you to abide by, if you did decide to accept my offer,' Lord Westcroft said slowly. She could see he wasn't sure if he had lost her to her racing thoughts.

'What terms?' It was best to know everything now, to have all the facts in her possession so she could make the best decision.

'I would ask you not to take a lover whilst I was alive.' He pressed his lips together and looked over her shoulder into the distance. 'It would complicate the matter of inheritance if you were to get pregnant.' She nodded, understanding his reasoning, and he quickly continued. 'I would leave you a generous settlement in my will. Enough to allow you to live as a wealthy widow for the rest of your life if you so desired, or to provide a generous dowry to take to your next marriage.'

His offer was kind, his tone calm but firm, and Alice realised he had thought about this a lot on his way to see her. What he was prepared to offer and what he wasn't. It showed how sure he was in his decisions and how convinced he was that he would likely go the same way as his father and his brother soon.

He fell silent and looked at her with those bright blue eyes, and she felt a pang of sadness that there was no desire in them now. What he was proposing was purely an arrangement made to safeguard her reputation and fulfil his obligation. He owed her nothing, but chivalry demanded he take responsibility for his part in tarnishing her reputation.

Alice turned away, desperately trying to weigh up what he was offering her. If she accepted his proposition she would be a countess, mistress of her own home and finally in charge of her own life. Yet she would live alone, with no prospect of love until Lord Westcroft died abroad and released her from the marriage.

She wanted children, a home filled with love, and this would give her none of that, but it would likely mean postponing that part of her life, not forgoing it.

The alternative was Cecil, if he would have her. After this scandal her parents would be more keen than ever to marry her off quickly and quietly, and she would be stuck with Cecil and his pawing hands and horrible views on society for the rest of her life.

'I could come with you,' she offered, turning back quickly. 'If you would prefer someone to look after you.'

'No,' he said sharply and then made an effort to soften his tone. 'I need to be alone. I can offer you my name and my protection, but no more, Miss James, not under any circumstance.'

'I understand,' she said. She would not build this into a fantasy of something that could never be. The decision had to be made on what he was offering, weighing that up with the alternative.

'I do not wish to rush you in your decision, but if we

are going to do this, it has to be quick for a couple of reasons. The first, as I said, I plan to be on a boat leaving London in two weeks, and the second is that rumours will spread fast. If we announce our engagement it will stop any malicious gossip in its tracks. You will be protected by your new title, but that only works if we pre-empt the majority of the speculation.'

'Your offer is very generous, Lord Westcroft,' Alice said, raising her eyes to meet his. 'I do not want you to feel obligated to do this. I never set out to trap you. I never thought this would be the culmination of last night.'

He smiled grimly. 'I know, Miss James. Perhaps we were both a little naïve thinking we could get away with such a deception. Please do not concern yourself with worrying that I might think you did this on purpose. I pride myself on being a good judge of character, and I like yours. If we had met in other circumstances, perhaps we would even have been friends.' He took her hand in his, and Alice inhaled sharply at the contact. 'I would not propose to a woman who I thought would bring my family's name into disrepute. I cannot make this decision for you, but please do not think I am insincere in what I am offering.'

Alice closed her eyes and let the two possible lives wash over her. The first was marriage to Cecil, a man she despised. The second was less conventional, perhaps a little lonely, but contained the chance of happiness along the way. She knew she had to be brave and reach out and grab what was being offered.

'Thank you, Lord Westcroft. I accept.'

Chapter Six

Simon adjusted his cravat and looked in the mirror. On the outside he looked composed and together, but inside he was less certain about what he was about to do. It was his wedding day, a day he had thought might never happen, yet here he was twelve days after proposing to Miss James, ready to get married.

It had been an odd couple of weeks. He had paused his preparations for leaving England, instead spending all his time preparing for his coming nuptials. Obtaining the special licence that allowed them to marry in haste had taken much time and a small fortune. Simon had called on friends throughout the country to exert their considerable influence and get one issued so quickly. It was a relief to know he would not have to change his plans after the wedding.

There was a knock on his door, and he glanced at the clock. There was still fifteen minutes until the ceremony, but he expected the vicar was already downstairs, preparing for the hurried nuptials.

'Come in,' he called, turning to face the door.

The door opened, and Sylvia, his youngest niece, slipped inside. She was six years old, a confident, happy child who managed to hold the whole family in her thrall despite her young age. She had only been one when her father died, and it saddened Simon that she would have no recollection of him at all.

'Good afternoon, little minx.'

She skipped into the room and threw herself down on the bed dramatically.

'Do you have to get married, Uncle?' she asked, clutching her doll to her chest. 'I don't want you to.'

'I have to get married,' Simon said, stopping what he was doing and coming to sit beside her. 'I would not be a very good person if I did not.'

'I wouldn't tell anyone you had been bad.'

'You might not tell anyone, but I would know.'

'What is she like? I probably won't like her.'

'Nonsense, Sylvia. I think you will like her very much.' He hid a grimace. He at least hoped so. Miss James seemed decent and kind, but he barely knew her. In the course of the last twelve days since he'd proposed, he had spent at most an hour in her company, the very minimum he could get away with. The truth was he didn't want to get to know Miss James. He didn't want to know her hopes and fears, her likes and dislikes. It would make leaving harder. This way Miss James remained a stranger, even if they would be married in an hour.

'Is she very pretty, like a princess?'

Simon considered. 'Yes, she is, although not as pretty as you, of course.'

Sylvia giggled and rolled her eyes. 'You have to say that. You're my uncle. Will you come and live with us, now you are to be married?' At present his sister-in-law and nieces lived in one of the many houses that made up the Westcroft estate. It was modest in size, plenty big enough for the growing children, but small enough to feel homely. Simon had offered Westcroft Hall to Maria and her children, insisting they need not move out of the home they had shared when Robert was alive, but his sister-in-law had refused, saying she could not bear to wake up in the bed she had shared with Robert every day, knowing she would never see his smile or feel his arms around her again. It meant Simon reluctantly had moved into Westcroft Hall, feeling as though he were stealing more of his brother's life from him.

'No, little minx,' he said with a sad smile. Of all the things he would miss about England, his nieces were at the top of the list. He loved the time he spent with them, the fun and laughter they brought to his life. They were one of the main reasons he had decided to go too. It was much better he fade from their memory, dead in a distant land, than they witness him expiring in front of them. That sort of thing scarred a person for life.

'I wish you would. I like it most of all when you are there, and I suppose I would learn to like Miss James.'

'Things will change these next few weeks, Sylvia,' he said, his tone serious. He hadn't told anyone of his plans yet, only Miss James who had been sworn to secrecy. Tomorrow he would bid farewell to his mother, his sister-in-law and his nieces before starting his journey south.

'I don't want things to change,' Sylvia said, her voice quiet, and he wondered if she had sensed something big was about to happen, something more than this sudden marriage to Miss James.

'I know it can be hard when things change, but you

must remember that you are surrounded by people who love you.'

Sylvia looked at him with her big eyes and nodded sadly, perhaps sensing there was more than what Simon was saying, more that would unsettle her.

'Sylvia, stop bothering your uncle,' Maria said as she bustled into the room. 'He has a wedding to prepare for.'

'I'm not bothering him. He likes my company,' Sylvia said, smiling cheekily at her mother.

'Go and find your sisters, Sylvia. I need to speak to your uncle in private.'

Sylvia pulled a face but slipped off the bed and left the room. Maria poked her head out the door after a few seconds to check she wasn't listening outside.

'Everything is ready downstairs,' she said, looking at him with concern. Everyone had been treating him like he had gone a little mad the last couple of weeks. The marriage they could understand, even if it was not ideal. He had been caught compromising the reputation of a young lady. Anyone who knew him would understand that he could not let the young woman in question suffer the consequences of their indiscretion alone, but it was the speed of the wedding that was a shock to his family. After delicate enquiries—which he quickly suppressed—as to whether Miss James was expecting a child, his friends and family had started to give him concerned looks all the time. He knew he could fix things by telling them of his plans, but he couldn't bear the burden it would place on them, knowing he too could follow in the path of his father and brother and expire any day.

'Are you sure you want to go through with this?' Maria asked, hovering near the door. 'There would be no shame in a longer engagement. It would allow you to get to know Miss James a little more. Surely that can only be a good thing.'

'Everything is arranged, Maria. The vicar is downstairs. This marriage needs to happen. What is the sense in delaying things?'

Maria bit her lip and stepped closer, laying a hand on his arm. 'If you told me you loved her, that you could not bear to spend a single moment apart from her, then I could understand the rush, but I do not think that is the case. You speak of Miss James with respect but not love.' She studied his face, and Simon felt as though she were looking into his soul. 'There is something more, isn't there?'

He swallowed, knowing if anyone was able to work out that he had been suffering with his headaches it would be Maria. She had watched her husband go through much the same, and he was worried she could see the same patterns emerging in him.

'Let us just enjoy the day,' he said, giving her a smile that he knew didn't reach his eyes.

Maria sighed but nodded, turning to leave.

'I wish you every happiness, Simon,' she said softly at the door. 'I know you think you do not deserve it, but you do.'

He stalled for a few more minutes before heading downstairs, a heavy weight in his stomach. Even though he didn't plan on sticking around to be part of this marriage he was entering into, it was still another person he was taking responsibility for. With one final check in the mirror, he tried to ignore the dark circles under his eyes and walked from his room.

* * *

Alice shifted nervously, wishing her mother would stop fussing and leave her alone. Her parents were understandably delighted by the turn of events; their daughter marrying an earl was beyond their wildest dreams.

It hadn't been all pleasant when she had first told them: they had been furious that she had allowed her reputation to be compromised, and only a visit from Lord Westcroft to assure Mr and Mrs James his intentions were now honourable could quieten their fears Alice would end up deserted and ruined.

Mrs James stepped back and admired her handiwork, tutted and then reached out to fiddle with Alice's hair again. They had been given one of the many bedrooms in Westcroft Hall for her to get ready in, and now Alice stood in the new dress that had been delivered a few days earlier, a gift from Lord Westcroft for their wedding day.

There was a soft knock on the door, and a moment later it opened and the dowager countess, Lord Westcroft's sister-in-law, entered the room.

'Mrs James, I think everything is almost ready downstairs. Perhaps you would like to take a seat with your husband.'

Mrs James flushed and curtsied clumsily, gave Alice a final look-over and then left the room.

The dowager countess smiled at Alice, her expression warm.

'How are you, my dear?'

'I feel as though I have a hundred frogs jumping inside my stomach,' Alice said and then flushed. It was probably too honest an answer.

'I remember my wedding day. I felt much the same. It

was a small affair in the local church, yet I felt as though the whole world was watching me.' She paused and then stepped closer. 'I know this has been thrust upon you both, but Lord Westcroft is a good man. He will do his duty by you and so much more.'

Alice looked away. Lord Westcroft's family were not aware of the nature of their impending marriage. They thought Alice and Lord Westcroft would live together as man and wife, not go their separate ways after the wedding, never to see one another again.

'You are kind, Lady Westcroft.'

She waved a hand. 'You must call me Maria. After today there will be three Lady Westcrofts. Simon's mother, me and now you. Let everyone else tie themselves up in knots working out who they are talking about, but we will be family and can be much more familiar.'

Alice felt the tears prick her eyes. These last few weeks she had felt bereft and uncertain in her decision. Her parents had been focussed on her elevation in status and what that meant for them. Lord Westcroft had been notably absent, sending her notes to update her on the progress of their impending wedding but only spending at most an hour with her in the last few weeks. It was comforting to have a friendly face, someone to make her think she might be welcomed into this family even if Lord Westcroft was not around to help her find her place.

'You will call me Alice?'

'I would be delighted to, Alice. Now, I do not know where you and Simon are planning on setting up your main residence, but whilst you are here in Northumberland we will take tea together at least once a week and go for long walks about the estate. I know how apprehensive you can feel, marrying into such a wealthy and influential family, and if there is anything I can do to help ease your path, you must tell me.'

'That is very kind, Maria.'

She smiled with a mischievous twinkle in her eye. 'Although, of course, I would not dream of interrupting you during the honeymoon period. Simon did not say if you were going away, but I expect he will at least take you on a tour of the residences he owns around the country.'

Alice dropped her gaze. Maria was a perceptive woman, and Alice sensed her future sister-in-law could tell there was something out of the ordinary about this marriage.

After a moment Maria let out an almost imperceptible sigh and then shrugged. 'I think it is time, Alice. Shall we make our way to the drawing room?'

Alice nodded and followed Maria out of the room, her eyes flitting over the dozens of portraits that lined the upstairs hallway. The house was old, with oak panelling in the main parts, with various wings and rooms added on at different points. It meant it had a haphazard charm and a mishmash of different styles throughout. They were in the oldest part here, built in Tudor times with sloping floorboards and walls that leaned first inward then outward. The walk felt as though it took for ever, even though it must have been less than thirty seconds between Alice leaving her room to getting downstairs.

They paused outside the drawing room, with Maria giving her one last squeeze of the hand before she slipped inside. For a moment Alice was left alone. She wondered if she was making a huge mistake. Lord Westcroft was a good man—she could tell that from the little time they had spent together—but she was not going to see him after they had sorted the practicalities of the next few days. She would be a countess, but a lonely one.

Alice squared her shoulders. She had chosen this path, and now she would follow it. The alternative had been worse, and now she had to find a way to make the life she had opted for bearable.

She ran her hands over the gold silk of the wedding dress, swallowing hard as she pushed open the door of the drawing room to see her future husband standing inside.

Chapter Seven

Ten months later

The house was quiet and dark as he approached, and he wondered if all the staff were in bed. It was late, much later than he had planned to arrive, but his ship had been delayed, and he had spent some time wandering the streets, trying to clear his head after the long and stormy voyage.

The last four days it had rained incessantly, a foreboding welcome back to England after nearly a year's absence. He had taken a boat from Italy, a journey that should have taken a little over two weeks, but because of the weather it had been much longer, and at one point he'd thought the captain was going to declare the trip a lost cause and turn around to seek shelter in one of the French ports.

Finally he had arrived home, uncertain how he felt to be back in London after his self-imposed exile.

He looked up at his townhouse and felt a wave of familiarity wash over him. His father had bought this house when Simon was a young boy, and he could remember visiting it for the first time, enthralled by all the sights and smells of London. His father had taken him by the hand and led him up the steps to the front door, then given him a tour of the house room by room, finishing up in the nursery at the very top. He'd pointed out the view over the square, the rooftops of London beyond, and Simon could remember feeling happy.

He'd spent much time there over the years, first with his parents when they travelled to London for the season, then when he was a young man Robert had given him free use of the house whenever he was in London. Since becoming the earl, Simon had been here even more, with his responsibilities often meaning he had to spend months at a time in London rather than in the wilds of Northumberland.

Before his departure to the Continent he had spent a long time ensuring there was enough supervision and funds to run all of his households without his oversight. He had not wanted to burden his mother or sister-in-law with the day-to-day questions that arose from owning a number of properties and employing the staff needed to keep everything running smoothly, so he had made sure there were senior household servants in each house he owned who were happy to take responsibility without the oversight of a master or mistress. He also employed a land steward and his assistant to collect rents and sort any queries from tenants and make decisions on the wider estate business.

Miss Stick was his trusted housekeeper of the London townhouse. Employed by the family for decades, she was a stiff and proper woman in her fifties with a good head for household accounts and just the right mix of authoritarian discipline and warmth to mean servants under her command were fiercely loyal and hardworking. No doubt, at half past midnight Miss Stick and the small complement of servants in the house were long asleep.

He had not sent word he was returning to England. Throughout his journey back he kept telling himself he would write to his mother, to Maria, to his steward to alert them of his plans to return to the country, but he never had. If he searched his soul he knew it was because he had wanted the chance to change his mind, even up until the boat docked and his feet touched English soil.

'Home,' he murmured as he touched the railing outside his house for the first time in many months. It was a strange feeling: for so long he had thought he would never see home again, convinced he would go to die in some foreign country surrounded by strangers. It was surreal to be back, and for much of the last few weeks he had felt as though he were floating through a dream.

He contemplated knocking at the door and decided against it, instead slipping round the side of the house and going through the gate into the small back garden. There were stairs here that led to the kitchen at basement level, and unless things had changed drastically he knew where Miss Stick hid the spare key.

A smile formed on his lips as he reached up to the lip above the door, his fingers closing around the cool metal of the key to the back door. He put it in the lock, turned it and slipped into the house.

Tomorrow it would be a surprise for the housekeeper to find him returned, but tonight at least the servants could sleep. There would be one bedroom at least kept ready for guests, for he was not the only person to use the house. Maria would often make the trip to London to visit friends and family, and less often his mother would too. He knew they weren't here now, though, for he had received a letter from his mother just before he had left Italy telling him that Maria and the children had just returned from London for the summer and that she was pleased to have them back in Northumberland.

Quickly he secured the door behind him and made his way through the kitchen and upstairs to the main part of the house. In the darkness everything looked the same as it always had, and he felt a sense of familiarity and comfort wash over him.

Upstairs he paused outside the bedroom door. There was a chance that his bedroom was not made up ready for someone to sleep in, but if that were the case he could check the others and choose one where the sheets were fresh to lie down on for the night.

He opened the door, surprised to find the room fresh and cool, a slight breeze blowing in through the open window. It was only open a crack, just enough to air the room and keep it at decent temperature despite the humidity outside. It was unlike Miss Stick to allow a window to stay open all night. She would normally cite the crime rate in this part of the city, figures Simon would not be able to refute but which seemed much higher than he would have imagined.

The curtains in the room billowed slightly with the breeze, and it took his eyes a moment to adjust to the darkness of the room. Outside, the moon was obscured by the heavy clouds that still threatened rain despite the days of downpours, and it was hard to see anything beyond the outline of the furniture. He took a few steps towards the large bed and felt the covers, relieved to find bed-sheets under his fingers. Quietly he closed the door and began to undress. His luggage would follow, and he was too weary to go digging through drawers to find any nightclothes so instead he stripped naked to the waist, throwing his clothes onto the chair that sat in the corner of the room, then gripped the bed-sheets and climbed into bed.

As soon as his body slipped between the sheets he knew something was wrong. There was a warmth there that shouldn't have been, the sort of warmth that can only come from a body. Tentatively he reached out, and his hand brushed against warm skin. For a moment he lingered, too shocked to move, and then he felt the person in his bed rolling over. Quickly he scrambled back, but it was too late. A hand shot out and grabbed hold of his wrist, and in the darkness he saw two wide eyes shining in an otherwise pitch-black room.

The woman screamed. It was the loudest sound he had ever heard, a scream filled with terror. He could not imagine anything more petrifying than finding someone else climbing into bed with you at night when you thought you were safe and alone in your room, so he did not blame her, but the sound pierced through him and made it impossible to reassure her.

From somewhere above he heard clattering as servants leaped out of their beds and rushed towards the stairs that would lead them here.

'I mean you no harm,' he said as calmly as he could muster. 'I am sorry.'

His words took a moment to penetrate the noise, but after a few seconds the screaming stopped and was replaced by a quiet whimpering.

'Miss James, is that you?'

'Yes,' she replied after a moment, scrambling to pull the bed-sheets up around her.

'My sincerest apologies. I did not know you would be in London.'

'No,' she murmured, 'I don't suppose you did.' There was a pause as she tried to compose herself, and then she said with more authority, 'It is not Miss James anymore, my Lord. You may have forgotten our marriage, but by law I am still Lady Westcroft.'

Her voice was cool, almost cold, and if the servants hadn't arrived at that very moment he thought she might go on to say more.

'My apologies, Lady Westcroft,' he said quietly.

'What is happening?' Miss Stick said as she rushed into the room, dressing gown billowing around her, cotton mob cap on her head. 'Lord Westcroft?'

Another servant, a maid he did not recognise, came rushing in behind Miss Stick followed by a young footman. The maid was holding a candle, and finally there was light in the room.

He surveyed the scene, a sinking feeling in his stomach. This was not how he had hoped his homecoming would unfold. He'd wanted to slip in, largely unobserved, and make quiet enquiries to bring himself up to date with the world he had left behind before everyone found out he was home. Instead probably every house on the square would know of his midnight return by the morning, no matter how firmly he pressed his servants on the need for discretion.

Simon breathed deeply and then adopted his most commanding tone.

'I am sorry to have disturbed you all. I thought to return without waking the whole household but was not aware Lady Westcroft was in residence.' Momentarily his eyes met his wife's, and then she looked away. 'Please return to your beds and go back to sleep.'

The maid and the footman turned immediately, but Miss Stick called out to stop them.

'The candle, Mary. You cannot expect Lord and Lady Westcroft to be left in the dark.'

The maid blushed and quickly placed the candle on the mantelpiece before curtsying and hurrying from the room.

Miss Stick waited until they had left and lowered her voice.

'The green room is also made up, my Lord, should you need it,' Miss Stick spoke with the practised discretion of a valued servant, making no assumptions, just letting him know the options available.

'Thank you, Miss Stick.'

'Do you need anything, my Lord? My Lady?'

'No, thank you,' he said, watching as the housekeeper turned to his wife. He was amazed to see her normally stern expression soften a little as Lady Westcroft smiled at her.

'No, thank you, Miss Stick. You have been wonderful as usual.'

The housekeeper's lips twitched, and he was surprised to realise she was almost smiling. Then she left the room, closing the door softly behind her.

For a long moment there was nothing but silence between them. The woman in front of him was a stranger, and he could see how invasive it was to have him climb half-naked into her bed. Yet he felt a flicker of irritation along with the regret at not checking the room was empty.

'It is late, Lord Westcroft,' she said, quietly but firmly. She was dressed in a cotton nightgown, and although it was not made of the most substantial material, it had a high neck and long sleeves that covered her modesty, yet she wrapped her arms about her in a way that made him realise she felt uncomfortable. He glanced down at his bare chest and hastily reached for his shirt, discarded on the chair.

'I will leave you to sleep, Lady Westcroft,' he said, gathering the rest of his clothes. 'My apologies again.' It felt strange to be leaving his bedroom, yet he would not think of throwing her out in the middle of the night. Instead he made a hasty retreat, closing the door on the stranger who was his wife.

Chapter Eight

Alice clasped her hands together to stop them from shaking as she paused outside the door to the dining room. Breakfast was normally one of her favourite times of the day. She loved taking her time over the first meal of the day, savouring her toast and eggs whilst she sipped on a steaming cup of delicious coffee. Miss Stick always ensured there was a newspaper ready and available for her to read, alternating between the more serious publications, which ensured she was informed about political and worldly matters, and the gossip sheets that meant she was never behind when it came to the intrigue of the *ton*. Since moving to London eight months previously, she had followed the same routine. Coffee, breakfast and half an hour with the newspaper before she was ready to face the day. It had been peaceful, but now her peace was shattered.

Straightening her back and lifting her chin, she pushed open the door and walked into the room, clenching her jaw as she saw Lord Westcroft was sitting in her favourite seat. It was the one at the head of the table, traditionally the master of the house's spot, but Alice had lived this past year with no husband and no master, and when she had decided to move her breakfast spot to the head of the table, there had been no one to object. That place was set in front of the large window and caught the best of the morning light.

Telling herself not to be so petty she forced a smile onto her face as Lord Westcroft looked up. He was holding her newspaper, the pages slightly crumpled in his hands.

'Good morning, Lady Westcroft. I hope you managed to sleep again after I disturbed you last night. My apologies again.'

'I did, thank you,' she lied. For hours she had lain in bed wondering what this sudden, unexpected return meant for her. Lord Westcroft hadn't deceived her when he had offered her marriage. He had been clear that he would not be there by her side as her husband, but she had not expected his departure to be so sudden, or so complete. One day after their wedding, he had left. Alice had known he had made plans to sail to the Continent but she had assumed he would escort her to her new home first, perhaps introduce her to the servants, be there as she got to know his mother and sister-in-law. A week, perhaps two—it wouldn't have needed long, but instead he had left without doing any of that. He had also made it clear his journey was one way and that she should not expect him back.

She took a seat at the dining table, looking up when Miss Stick came into the room, a frown on her face when she saw Lord Westcroft sitting in Alice's accustomed place, reading her newspaper. Alice felt a rush of warmth for the housekeeper. She had been terrified of her when she had first arrived in London and almost made the decision to flee back to Northumberland, but slowly she had won the housekeeper round, making an ally out of the older woman.

'Good morning, Lady Westcroft. I will tell Cook to make you a fresh cup of coffee and get started on your eggs. Is there anything else you need this morning?'

'No, thank you, Miss Stick. Join me in the drawing room after breakfast, and we can discuss the meals for the week.'

Miss Stick inclined her head and left the room. Alice felt her husband's eyes on her and turned to him.

'If you would be so kind as to inform me of your plans, Lord Westcroft, insofar as planning the meals and social calendar for the week goes, I would appreciate it.'

He looked at her as if she had grown a second head.

'Social calendar?' he murmured.

She held up a hand and counted off on her fingers, 'I have a number of events planned this week. Afternoon tea with the London Ladies' Benevolent Society, dinner parties with the Hampshires and the Dunns, and a fund-raising event at the end of the week. It would be helpful to know if you will be here or not.'

'You live here?' he asked, puzzlement on his face.

'Yes,' she said, slowly.

'In London?'

'Yes.'

'In this house?'

'Where would you prefer I live, my Lord?'

He rallied, and she silently chided herself for her frosty tone, but the situation was impossible. She had made a life for herself here. It had been far from easy, and it had taken months to build the social circle she had now, but it had been worth it. Now that Lord West-croft was back, his purpose as yet undeclared, she felt as though he might suddenly pull it all away from her.

'I thought you were in Northumberland.'

'I spent a few months in Northumberland after we married, then I moved to London.'

'No one said, in their letters.'

Alice looked away, glad when the maid bustled in with a plate of eggs and toast and a steaming pot of coffee.

She hadn't written to Lord Westcroft: there had hardly seemed a point. Her husband was a stranger, a man she had spent very little time with before they were married and even less after. She knew his mother had written detailed letters telling him about the family and the estate, and so had Maria, but she had asked both not to include her in their letters. They had complied, seeing her discomfort of her new position and wanting to do anything to help her feel accepted and settled.

Lord Westcroft waited until they were alone again and then fixed her with an unwavering stare. 'I know it must be a shock, my turning up like this with no warning.'

'It is,' Alice said, buttering her toast a little more vigorously than she normally would. 'But it is your home. I do not know why I am surprised.'

'Perhaps because I told you I was leaving and never coming back,' he said gently.

Alice put down her knife. She could feel the tension in every muscle of her body. For twenty-one years she had not been in control of her own life. She had lived by her parents' rules, tied to the fate they determined for her, and then suddenly she had been granted her freedom. Lord Westcroft had given her a great gift, she knew that, and her coolness towards him now was only because she feared she might lose that freedom. She exhaled slowly, suppressing the uncertainty and the fear, and turned to her husband.

'How are you?' she said, studying him properly. 'It is good to see you looking so well.'

Simon felt the weight of her scrutiny. Her eyes took their time as she looked over his face and body. He knew what she would see, something entirely unexpected: a man who had gone away to die looking healthier and stronger than ever before.

'I am well,' he said quietly. 'At least, I think I am.'

'You think…?'

He sighed heavily and glanced out the window to where the sunshine was reflecting off the puddles that lay on the street. It had been a difficult truth to come to terms with, almost as difficult as thinking he was dying.

'I told you of my father and brother, their headaches, their sudden deaths,' he said, hoping he would not have to go through the painful history again.

'Yes, I remember, and your mother told me a little more after we were married, after you left.'

'Yes, she suffered terribly. First her husband, then her eldest son. Both struck down in their prime when they had young families to care for.'

'When you left you were getting awful headaches,' Lady Westcroft prompted gently. 'It was the reason you were so keen to leave so quickly.'

'I'd been having them for some time on a daily basis. I'd consulted two reputable doctors, and after listening to the story of my father and brother they both told me the same thing.' He paused, remembering the first time a doctor had looked him in the eye and told him he was going to die. 'They told me in all likelihood I would be dead before the year was out.'

'They couldn't have known that,' she murmured, shaking her head.

'They spoke of a malformation of the vessels in the brain, a condition that runs in families. Apparently it has been seen in cadavers when they have undergone dissection for medical training. Evidence of a catastrophic bleed in the brain and a story of headaches before death.'

She looked away, her fork pushing the egg around on her plate before she laid it down and picked up her cup of coffee, cradling it with both hands.

'They told you that was what would happen to you?'

'Yes.'

'That's terrible.'

'At the time I felt like it only confirmed my suspicions.'

She took a sip of coffee and then looked over at him. 'Yet you're still here and look as healthy as a man in his prime.'

'When I left I was having daily headaches, but over the next few months they gradually dwindled.'

He had been unable to believe it at first, thinking it was perhaps just a short reprieve, but as he had travelled farther from England, his headaches had become fewer. He'd settled in a remote part of Italy, high in the Tuscan hills. It was beautiful there, and for the first time in a long time he had felt at peace.

'When I had been in Italy for two months I sought the advice of an eminent physician in Florence. I explained my symptoms and what had happened to my father and my brother. He told me it was not yet my time to die.'

Lady Westcroft's eyes widened, and she had a look of incredulity on her face. 'Did he explain the headaches?'

Simon shifted uncomfortably. 'He said they were likely caused by the huge amount of stress I was under, imagining myself dying.' For some reason it felt uncomfortable to admit it, that he had brought the headaches on himself. 'He told me it was self-perpetuating. The first time I got a headache I thought it must be the start of the same condition they had died from. The stress of that thought meant I woke every day with a headache that would not relent.'

'It is easy to see how that could happen,' Lady Westcroft said. Now she had lost her frostiness towards him, she seemed more like the reasonable young woman he had proposed to. He watched her as she sipped her coffee. He was ashamed to admit he had not thought much about her this past year. His guilt had been over leaving his mother and sister-in-law behind, along with his young nieces. They had been the reason he had returned, not the wife he had almost forgotten about.

It was only a year ago he had left, a little less, yet he realised Lady Westcroft *had* changed. Not physically, at least not at first glance, but there was something about her manner, a poise and confidence that she hadn't had before. When they had married she had seemed overwhelmed by the wealth and status of the family she was marrying into, yet now she sat in this dining room confident in her role as mistress of the house. He even thought he'd seen her eyeing his chair at the head of the table when she'd entered.

'I am truly glad you are not dying, Lord Westcroft,' she said softly.

'Thank you. So am I.' He paused, deciding to be entirely candid with her. 'The doctor in Italy said there was a good possibility I had the same condition as my father and brother, that he could not guarantee I would not be plagued by the headaches that were the harbinger of a sudden death, but he urged me to resume my life and said it might happen in a year or in forty years.'

'So here you are,' Lady Westcroft said.

'Here I am.'

She glanced at the clock on the mantelpiece and put down her cup of coffee. Her breakfast lay barely touched on her plate.

'I am sure you are still finalising your plans, my Lord,' she said, standing and dropping into a formal little curtsy. 'When you have decided what you will be doing and where you will be staying, please let me know. Now I must leave you. I have an engagement I forgot about.'

Before he had a chance to answer, she turned and hurried out the room. He had the sense she was escaping him, running away from having to interact with him anymore. Leaning back in his chair he laced his fingers together in front of his chest. At least he had begun the conversation between them. Throughout his voyage home he had avoided thinking too much of his accidental wife. In his mind she was living quietly in one of his properties in Northumberland, taking long country walks and occupying herself with needlework or watercolours. He'd thought he would have time before he told her the circumstances of their marriage had changed, that she was no longer wife to an absent husband. He'd imagined arranging a time to meet as they discussed how their lives would continue now he was home. With a groan he remembered instead how he had climbed into bed with her after a year of no contact whatsoever. Never would he be able to rid himself of the terrified look on her face or the awful scream as she saw him in the darkness.

He sighed. It was a lot for her to take in, yet all he wanted was to reassure her. In the main her life need not change. There was no requirement for them to live as husband and wife, even if he were in the country. She could stay at one property, he another. Lady Westcroft was a sensible woman; he may have only known her for a short time, but he had been able to tell that from their acquaintance before their marriage. She was sensible, and he was sure with a little time she would see their arrangement could continue without too much disruption.

For a second he thought back to the kiss they had shared in the garden of Lady Salisbury's party on Midsummer's Eve the year before. It had been a magical moment, and for a few minutes he had allowed himself to imagine a different future.

Quickly he shook his head. It wasn't to be. He had decided long ago he was never going to marry or have children. He had broken his first vow when his hand had been forced after meeting the now Lady Westcroft that fateful Midsummer's Eve, but that didn't mean he had to change his whole life's philosophy.

Chapter Nine

Alice looked round the room in satisfaction. There was a low hum of chatter and everyone was smiling and seeming to have a good time. The London Ladies' Benevolent Society had been established long before she had arrived in London, but she had found them a lacklustre group of four elderly women of the upper-middle class who had good intentions but not much idea as to how to implement them. In the last six months, since she had taken the helm of the society, it had gone from strength to strength. They now had regular monthly meetings, the location of which rotated between the homes of the more influential members, and held fundraising activities every couple of months too. Alice was well aware that initially many of the ladies had only agreed to be part of it so they could get the measure of her, the mysterious new countess that no one knew anything about, but she hoped that now they saw the benefits of a well-run society that could help them focus their philanthropic efforts.

She took a sip of tea and tried to focus on what Lady Kennington was saying as she rapped earnestly on the arm of the sofa with her fan.

'It just is not good enough. These poor orphans are dressed in rags, given gruel to eat and not even taught their letters or numbers, then society acts surprised when they go on to be the next generation of beggars and criminals. There needs to be better provision for them.'

'There is not endless money, though, Lady Kennington,' Mrs Taylor said. She was a wealthy widow who donated both her time and money generously. Alice was pleased at how she had chipped away at the hierarchical structure these last few months. She'd wanted all members to feel they had a voice, an opinion, whether they be duchess or doctor's wife.

'No, there is not. Yet I wonder whether the conditions the poor orphans find themselves in isn't at least a little deliberate. There is a large proportion of society who think people should stay within their own social status. We have all seen how the self-made man is snubbed at society events, even when he is the wealthiest in the room.'

'Do you have a solution, Lady Kennington?' Alice asked. A few months ago she would have worried that there was an unspoken agenda when there was talk of people staying within their own social class, but she had learned it was best to act oblivious to people's opinions. If they never saw you react, they soon got bored and started talking about someone else.

'St Benedict's Home for Orphaned Children,' Lady Kennington announced with a triumphant smile. 'A small orphanage near the slums of St Giles. I think they have beds for twelve girls and twelve boys. At the moment it is in the poorest part of the city, and the children are lucky to reach their fourteenth birthday, when they are thrown back out on the streets.'

'I think I know the one you mean,' Alice said, thinking of the dilapidated building that looked as though it would collapse with the slightest gust of wind.

'We cannot intervene everywhere, but I propose we invest some of our funds there. Make a difference for those twenty-four children and use them as a study to present to Parliament to show the benefits to all society if we look after the poorest amongst us.'

Alice felt a shiver run through her at the idea. More than anything she wanted to make a difference for children. It had been hard coming to terms over the last year with the fact that she would not have children of her own, at least not anytime soon. She had begun to build a relationship with her beautiful nieces, the three children her sister-in-law had gracefully helped her bond with, and she had also recently returned from a short trip to see her own sister and little nephew. She could surround herself with children to love even if she could have none of her own yet, but she also wanted to make a difference to some of the orphaned and destitute children of London. The unwavering support of someone as influential as Lady Kennington would mean projects like St Benedict's Orphanage were much more likely to become success stories.

She was surprised when the door opened and Lord Westcroft walked into the room. He in turn looked stunned by two dozen women crowded into his drawing room, and Alice saw him stiffen and then glance over his shoulder, but it was too late. He had been spotted.

'Lord Westcroft,' Lady Kennington called, beaming at

him. 'You have returned from your travels.' She turned to Alice and said admonishingly, 'You should have told us, my dear. This is exciting news.'

No one else noticed the fraction of a second's hesitation before Lord Westcroft smiled indulgingly and stepped into the room as if he had always planned to spare a few minutes of his time with the ladies. He moved between groups of people smoothly, greeting old acquaintances and bowing to new ones, and Alice watched in wonder as he left each group beaming with pleasure at the small snippet of attention he bestowed upon them. He went round the room before approaching Alice and her little group, greeting Lady Kennington and speaking warmly to Mrs Taylor.

'This is quite the gathering, Lady Westcroft,' he said, looking around.

'Hard to believe six months ago the London Ladies' Benevolent Society was four elderly women and a small pot of donations,' Lady Kennington said, patting Alice on the hand. 'Lady Westcroft has done a marvellous job at getting everyone so interested and invested in the society.'

Lord Westcroft smiled politely and then turned to Alice. 'I hate to take you away from your gathering, but there are one or two things we need to discuss quickly. Shall we step outside?'

Lady Kennington chuckled under her breath and leaned into Mrs Taylor. 'I remember that first blush of love. Only back a day and already he's finding excuses to pull his wife aside.'

Alice didn't respond but stood, smoothing her skirt, and followed Lord Westcroft from the room.

The London house was a good size for a townhouse, but it wasn't large compared to Lord Westcroft's other residences. Downstairs there was the drawing room, the dining room, another small, cosier reception room and Lord Westcroft's study. The study was the only room in the house she had never made herself at home in. It had felt too personal somehow, even though until yesterday she had been under the impression Lord Westcroft was never going to return.

He led her into the study now, closing the door quietly behind him.

'There are a lot of women in our drawing room,' he said.

'I think I mentioned the meeting of the London Ladies' Benevolent Society.'

'I expected something…different.' He leaned against the edge of the desk, his posture relaxed, and the expression on his face one of curiosity rather than annoyance. She had been well aware that he would be surprised by the invasion of his home by twenty-four benevolently minded women and hadn't known how he would take it. She was pleasantly surprised to find he wasn't angry or ordering everyone out, merely curious. 'You came to London less than a year ago for the first time ever?'

'Yes.'

'You knew no one?'

She shook her head.

'Yet here you are, with some of the wealthiest women in England taking tea in our drawing room.'

'You left, my Lord,' Alice said, holding up a hand to stall the interruption she knew was coming. 'I am not placing any blame. You told me exactly what would happen once we were married, but I do not think I had truly understood. I was alone, completely alone. Independent, wealthy, no longer obliged to do what my parents wanted of me. Yet I was lost.'

He shifted, and for a moment Alice thought he might reach out and take her hand. She chided herself at the surge of anticipation she felt at the idea, especially when he merely crossed one leg over the other and rested his hand back on the edge of the desk.

'I could either sit in one of your houses in Northumberland, waiting for you to die so my life could start again, or I could choose to build something for myself now. The first option was just too depressing so I chose the second.'

There was silence for a moment, and she glanced up at his face, relieved to see he was smiling, albeit sadly. 'I left you with quite the dilemma. Please do not misconstrue my intentions in speaking with you now. I am impressed, not annoyed. I think it is a miracle you have managed to get society to accept you so readily, let alone chair a benevolent charity.'

'You do not mind the twenty-four women sitting in your drawing room?'

He grimaced and then shrugged. 'It is not what I would have chosen for my first day back in London, but I acknowledge I did not give you any notice of my return so it would be unreasonable for you to keep the house quiet and not have social plans.' Lord Westcroft paused, looking at her intently before continuing. 'I am keen to discuss our situation and how we will manage things going forward, though.'

Alice felt a bubble of nerves deep inside. She wondered if he would expect her to remove herself to the countryside. So far since returning, he had been polite but distant. She was fast realising that she was still an afterthought in his life. Whatever his reasons for coming back to England, she was not one of them. Alice tried not to be hurt by the realisation she was once again close to the bottom of his list of priorities. She prided herself on being a rational woman and knew Lord Westcroft had given her so much when he married her to protect her reputation, so it felt ungrateful to want him to think more of her, yet it hurt when she felt like a problem to be solved.

She turned away, needing a moment to compose herself. When she turned back it was with steely determination. This might be Lord Westcroft's house, but she had worked hard this last year to find her footing in London, and she wasn't going to scurry back to Northumberland just because it made his life a little more convenient and allowed him to forget he had a wife. If he found it too uncomfortable to be here with her, then he could leave, but she was not going to quietly give up everything she had built for herself these last few months.

'I shall look at my calendar, my Lord,' she said, ensuring her tone was polite and courteous. 'Now, if you will excuse me, I must return to my guests.'

She didn't wait for his response, turning and leaving the study quickly and closing the door behind her. As she walked back through the hall she realised her hands were shaking, and she paused for a moment before re-entering the drawing room, fixing her face into a warm and happy expression that she didn't quite feel.

'Good Lord, Westcroft, you leave the country to die and come back looking healthier than the rest of us put together,' William Wetherby said as he clapped Simon on the back. Wetherby was an old friend, their friendship forged in the difficult days when they had both been sent away to school. Wetherby had been a scrawny lad from a once-wealthy family that had fallen on hard times. He'd had his place at Eton paid for by a generous aunt but had been mercilessly teased about his old clothes and lack of funds to spend in the local town.

Now Wetherby had grown into a giant of a man, broad across the chest with a thick dark beard and a muscular build. He was no longer poor either, having spent the last decade building up a thriving importing business.

Simon smiled, a little surprised at how pleased he felt to see his old friend. When he had left England he had thought it would be the last time he saw anyone he knew. At the time, he had told himself he'd made his peace with that, but now he realised that wasn't the case.

'It is good to see you, Wetherby,' Simon said, accepting the embrace his old friend pulled him into. Wetherby had always been effusive, and the years hadn't changed him in that respect.

There were a few other men gathered nearby who greeted him and shook his hand. London society was made up of a relatively small number of people, and even the men he did not know well he was acquainted with. After a minute Wetherby guided Simon to a corner table and motioned for a couple of drinks to be brought over.

In his youth Simon had not enjoyed the atmosphere in the exclusive gentlemen's club that his father and brother had attended and his membership was expected, but as he had grown older he had come to appreciate the quiet, luxurious atmosphere the club afforded. It was a place to escape many of the demands made on his time, and when he needed it to, it allowed him to spend an hour or so alone with his thoughts.

'I find myself fearful to enquire after your health,' Wetherby said as they sat facing each other.

Not many people knew of the terrible headaches Simon had suffered before he left England, nor the fear he had harboured that the headaches were a sign he would soon die, but he had taken Wetherby into his confidence when he sought his help with obtaining the special licence for his marriage almost a year earlier. Wetherby had worked tirelessly, calling in favours from various friends and acquaintances, to make sure Simon could marry before he left England.

'The headaches have all but gone. A doctor in Florence tells me it is not my time to leave this earth just yet.'

'That is a relief.' Wetherby eyed him cautiously. 'So you are back for good?'

For a long moment Simon didn't answer. It was a question he had put off thinking about throughout his trip home. When it became apparent his headaches were abating, he had been left unsure what to do. The doctor in Florence had been clear he wasn't giving Simon the reassurance that he wouldn't one day succumb to the same condition that had killed his father and brother, just the likelihood that it wouldn't be yet. For a few months after this news, Simon had stalled, trying to enjoy the solitude in his remote Tuscan villa, but all the while, home had been calling.

He had wanted to see his mother and sister-in-law, to receive the bear hugs he loved so much from his nieces and see how they had grown. He felt a deep unease at abandoning his responsibilities and the need to remove the burden he had placed on so many when he had left. More than all of that, to his surprise, was this burning desire to be home. Italy was beautiful and peaceful, but he felt the pull of the familiar.

Yet now he was back, he needed to decide what the future would look like. The likelihood that one day he would die suddenly and violently hadn't changed, it was merely the time frame that had been altered in his mind. He still didn't want anyone he loved to witness his death, and that would mean keeping his distance, yet his heart called for the opposite.

He shifted uncomfortably in his chair. Then there was the question of his wife. He pushed the thought aside. Lady Westcroft made an already complicated situation even more difficult to untangle.

'At least for a while. I will head to Northumberland soon. I wanted to reacclimatise myself to life in England before heading back home, but I should see the family soon.'

'I expect you wanted to see your wife too,' Wetherby said, his eyes flicking up to examine Simon's expression.

'In truth I did not realise she was in London.'

'She has been here for quite a time now. Lady Westcroft has made a significant impression on London society.'

Simon raised an eyebrow. It was clear what his friend said was true: his wife had a busy social calendar and chaired a benevolent society despite arriving in London a mere eight months earlier with no friends and no connections.

'You have met her?'

'Of course. I invited her to share my box at the opera just last week,' Wetherby said as he leaned forward. 'She is your countess, Westcroft, although I hasten to give her credit for the impression she has made. People gave her a chance because you married her, but she has grasped hold of that chance and charmed everyone at every opportunity.'

'It does seem as though she has been busy.' He thought back to the wide-eyed, uncertain girl he had met at the masquerade ball. No one could deny the change in his wife since then, and perhaps it was to be expected. He had left her to fend for herself, and she had thrived. He was pleased for her—the last thing he wanted was for her to be unhappy—but he felt a little uncomfortable too, although if he was asked to articulate why, he would have found it difficult.

'You will take her back to Northumberland with you?'

'I will ask, but I get the impression Lady Westcroft has a full social calendar these next few weeks.'

Wetherby laughed. 'I expect she does. Her company is very much in demand.'

Simon felt a flicker of guilt. There was a lot to feel guilty about with respect to his wife. He'd married her and then abandoned her, and even though he had been completely honest with her before their marriage, he had known that she wouldn't have quite understood the realities of the change in her circumstance. Now he had this horrible feeling that he had trapped her. The deal he had promised her was a short marriage to save her reputation, followed by the freedom of widowhood. She would be wealthy enough to make her own decisions and, after a short period of mourning, could either cultivate a life as a wealthy widow or start to look for a second husband, someone she could share a full and proper marriage with.

He swallowed hard, covering the movement by raising his glass to his lips. He had the sense that he had stolen her life away from her and as yet she wasn't quite aware of it. If he lived for another forty years she would be trapped in this union, never experiencing a love match, never getting to have children of her own. It was not what he had promised her.

He took another gulp of his drink before setting the glass down on the table. Somehow they would find a way through this mess, but he had an overwhelming feeling that he had deceived Lady Westcroft. Never had he pressed her to marry him, only laid it out as an option, but he wasn't sure she would have accepted if she had known it would mean being tied to him for an indeterminate amount of time, unable to move on with a life of her own.

'How are you, Wetherby?' Simon asked, wanting to change the subject, needing the distraction of talking about something else for a while.

'I am well, thank you. I leave in a few weeks for a trip to Africa. I hear the earth is littered with diamonds in places, and I want to see for myself whether this is true.'

Simon grinned. His friend had always had difficulty staying in one place for too long, and every few years would announce a new voyage. Wetherby had shaken off the bad luck that had made him an easy victim during their schooldays and seemed to find success in each of his ventures. Even if the ground wasn't littered with diamonds, no doubt there would be some opportunity his friend would spot and bend to his advantage.

'I must leave you,' Wetherby said, standing and clapping him on the shoulder. 'We should talk properly, perhaps when you are back from Northumberland, but today I have a prior engagement with an architect.' He leaned in closer. 'The chap is a genius, and I'm trying to persuade him to take time away from his other projects to build me a nice little house in the Sussex countryside.'

'I wish you luck,' Simon said, rising and shaking Wetherby's hand.

He was left alone with his thoughts, wondering how to make things right with Lady Westcroft, but aware that short of dying there was no way of delivering the life he had promised her.

Chapter Ten

Simon had risen early, keen to busy himself with some of the many things he had neglected in the time he had been away. He had spent much of the morning going over correspondence that had been kept for him whilst he was in Italy and then around lunchtime had met with his solicitor to discuss some minor legal issues that needed his input. Although he had not consciously sought to avoid Lady Westcroft, he was aware that he had organised his morning so their paths were unlikely to cross.

Now that he was walking home he had a sinking feeling in his stomach. It wasn't that he disliked his wife— far from it. Despite hardly knowing her he felt certain she was good and kind, a sweet young woman who had thrived in difficult circumstances. In a way, that made what he was doing to her even worse. His return had once again thrown her life into turmoil.

Simon slowed as he approached the Serpentine. He had decided to take the longer route through the park back to his townhouse, enjoying the warmth of the early-summer afternoon and also feeling a need to delay his return when he might have to sit and have a serious discussion with his wife about their futures.

As he paused to look at the water, a group of about a dozen ladies seated on the grass a little way from its edge caught his eye. They were finely dressed and as he looked closer he realised he recognised one or two, his eyes sweeping over the group until they settled on the pretty, petite form of his wife. She was dressed in dark blue, a colour that served to accentuate the red in her hair and the beautiful porcelain paleness of her skin. She looked relaxed, leaning back on her hands as she turned her head to talk to the woman next to her.

None of the ladies had spotted him, and so for a moment he just watched Lady Westcroft. She was mesmerising. It was undeniable she was pretty, but that quality became enchanting when she smiled. The smile was natural and easy on her lips, and Simon felt himself drawn to her as he had been on the night of the masquerade ball. He wanted to stride over and pull her into his arms, tracing the softness of her face with his fingers, making it so her smile was directed at only him.

It was an unsettling feeling, and quickly he tried to dampen it. The last thing he needed now was to feel attraction towards his wife. He needed a clear head in the negotiations that were to come about their future, and feeling desire for the woman whose life he was ruining would not help.

As he watched, two young children ran up to the group, talking excitedly to the woman who sat beside Lady Westcroft. The boy had a model boat in his hand and was gesticulating at the Serpentine. Their mother laughed indulgently, but it was Lady Westcroft who stood and took the boy's hand, allowing him to lead her down to the water. She crouched down in between the little boy and girl, listening intently to what they said and then helped them set the boat on the water. On the first attempt it wobbled and nearly capsized, and he found himself smiling as Lady Westcroft threw her head back and laughed alongside the children. The second attempt was more successful, and they stayed watching the boat as it bobbed along in the water.

Simon felt a pang of sadness, both for himself and his wife. He could see by this simple interaction how good Lady Westcroft was with children. Despite not spending the time to get to know her hopes and dreams for the future, he could remember her talking of the idea of children fondly and this being the main concern when weighing up whether she should accept his proposal for the marriage to save her reputation.

At the time, the offer he had made called for her to postpone her desire for a family, but now, with the question of his mortality very much unclear, it might be that Lady Westcroft would never have children of her own.

Simon was about to turn away when his wife glanced up, looking directly at him. For a moment she did not move and then she stood, inclining her head in an invitation for him to join her.

With a sinking heart he walked over slowly. In all this mess he could not deny his own disappointment, even though he felt guilty for even considering trying to live a normal life. Once, long before he had lost his brother, he had assumed he would marry and have a family of his own. Now he knew that would never happen, and even though he'd had years to get used to the idea, sometimes he yearned for a normal life. Then he felt guilty for being so selfish when he was lucky to be alive while his brother was not.

'Lord Westcroft, I did not expect to see you here in the park,' Lady Westcroft said. She spoke warmly although addressed him formally. He was once again impressed at how much she had learned these last few months in London. Not only had she gained the support of the most influential in society, she had quickly refined her country manners that might make her stand out as different.

'I had an appointment with my solicitor and thought I would take the scenic route home. It is a beautiful afternoon.'

'It is indeed. We were meant to meet at Mrs Lattimer's for tea, but no one could resist when she suggested an outing to the park instead.' Lady Westcroft motioned behind her to the woman she had been sitting next to.

Simon looked round, nodding in greeting to the ladies he was acquainted with. They were watching him with open curiosity, no doubt keen to see how he interacted with the wife he had left behind after a single day of marriage.

'I do not want to disturb you.'

She looked up at him with a half-smile on her face. When he had left ten months earlier, she had seemed young and innocent; now there was an air of experience in her poised demeanour, and Simon knew he was responsible for forcing her to grow up.

'It is good to see you, my Lord. I have hardly set eyes on you since you returned to England.'

Simon attempted to smile but struggled to produce more than a twitch of his lips, surprised again at how forgiving his wife seemed. He'd abandoned her in a world she did not know, and now he was threatening to rock the life she had made for herself again.

'Shall we take a little stroll? I am sure Sebastian and Lilith will not mind.' With natural ease Lady Westcroft crouched down and swept the model boat from the water, handing it back to Sebastian. 'We do not want it to sail out into the middle of the lake. I do not relish the idea of wading out to fetch it.'

Sebastian giggled and then wrapped his chubby arms around her neck. Simon watched as his wife's face flushed with joy. Lady Westcroft waited until the two children were safely back in the care of their nanny before she turned her attention back to Simon.

'They are sweet children,' she said with a smile as she followed his gaze before lowering her voice. 'Sometimes I find myself envious of their nanny. I am sure behind closed doors they are sometimes a terror, but you would not believe it when you see them in public.'

'Have you had a pleasant day?'

'Yes, thank you. I spent some time going through the household accounts with Miss Stick this morning. A mere formality, as she is the most organised of housekeepers I have ever met, but I like to learn how to do these things, and she is a good teacher. Then this afternoon has been spent in the sunshine with friends.'

'It does sound a nice way to spend an afternoon,' Simon murmured.

She looked at him curiously. 'I do have a good life, my Lord. I am aware how lucky I am.'

So much hung unsaid between them, and Simon knew they would have to address it soon, but he didn't want to do that here with everyone watching them. What he had to say would be better received in private where Lady Westcroft would have the freedom to react without having to think of who was watching.

They walked a little farther along the path, arm-in-arm. Half her face was in shadow from the bonnet that was tied firmly under her chin, and it made it difficult to work out what she might be thinking.

Simon wished for a moment that this was their life, an easy happiness where all they had to worry about was which social invitations to accept and which to refuse. Quickly he pushed the thought away. The idea of a conventional marriage to Lady Westcroft was tempting as he walked beside her. She was kind and sensible and pleasant to be around. He couldn't deny the flicker of desire he felt every time she looked at him with those blue eyes or the way something clenched deep inside him when she smiled. Yet it was a temptation he could never give in to. It would be unfair, with his future so uncertain. It would be better to offer her a deal where they both led separate but contented lives, only occasionally meeting.

As if sensing his thoughts, she turned to face him again, her eyes rising to meet his. 'You seem troubled, my Lord.'

He cleared his throat but couldn't find the words.

'Is something amiss?'

'I watched you for a moment with those children. You were very good with them.'

'I like children.'

'I know.'

She held his gaze, something defiant in her eyes as if pushing him to confront the big issue that stood between them.

'Would you like children, Lady Westcroft?' The question came out much more directly than he meant it to, but with her standing so close he felt as if his thoughts were all scrambled.

It took her a moment to reply, and when she did her tone was much more formal. 'I understand the limits of our marriage, Lord Westcroft, and I am not a naïve girl any more. I understand a marriage has to be consummated for there to be children.' Her cheeks flushed as she spoke, and he felt like a cad.

'Forgive me, I did not meant to cause you pain. I...' He was unsure how to put into words the turmoil he felt inside. It was impossible to know how to tell Lady Westcroft that because of his mistake in making the assumption that he was dying, he had stolen from her the future he had promised.

She turned away, but before she did, he saw the tears glistening in her eyes.

'I must return to my friends, my Lord,' she said, already beginning to move away. 'Perhaps I shall see you at home later this evening.'

He inclined his head, watching her as she walked back to the group of ladies a little distance away. As he turned to leave he felt a wave of guilt almost consume him. He needed space and time, some way to come up with a plan where no one suffered too much. Here in London, he felt as though everything was pressing in, threatening to crush him.

It was growing dark outside when Alice sat down to see to her mound of correspondence. She had a letter from each of her nieces to reply to, each of different lengths dependent on their ages, and one from Maria as well. She wondered if her sister-in-law knew of Lord Westcroft's return and realised she shouldn't be the one to tell her. No doubt her husband would contact his family soon, if he hadn't already. Gossip travelled at an unbelievable pace, and he had been seen by half the wealthy women in London that afternoon when he had stumbled upon Alice and her friends in Hyde Park. It might be hundreds of miles to the Westcroft estate in Northumberland, but the news of his return would be up there before the month was out.

She enjoyed the ritual of letter-writing and took her time selecting her pen and positioning the paper, ensuring she had good candlelight so as not to strain her eyes.

As she was about to put pen to paper she paused, hearing footsteps in the hallway outside and then a knock on the door. She turned to see Miss Stick entering, holding something in her hand.

'Lord Westcroft asked me to give this to you, my Lady,' Miss Stick said. The older woman was always polite and formal, but Alice had gone to great efforts to get to know the housekeeper in recent months. She could see something was wrong and took the letter in trepidation.

She was puzzled to see her husband's seal on the back and glanced up at Miss Stick briefly.

'I am sorry, my Lady. He left about an hour ago.'

With a sinking feeling she opened the note and let her eyes skim over the words. It was brief, only a couple of sentences, explaining he needed to go and see his family, to tell them he was back before the gossip reached them. There was no indication of when he might come back to London, just an apology for leaving so soon.

For a second she slumped, feeling rejected once again, then forced herself to rally.

'Lord Westcroft has gone,' she said to Miss Stick. 'There is no word as to when he will return. I expect he will stay in Northumberland for some time.'

Miss Stick's expression softened slightly, and then she nodded and held Alice's eye. 'There will be no change to your plans then, my Lady? Everything will continue as normal?'

'Everything will continue as normal,' Alice confirmed.

Once she was alone Alice allowed her control to slip and slumped in her chair. He hadn't even bothered to say goodbye. She could justify his behaviour all she liked, but that was hard to bear. She understood he would have been keen to return to his family, to be the one to tell them he was back in the country so they weren't surprised by the information from someone else, yet it would only have taken a few minutes to bid her farewell.

She thought back to their conversation that afternoon and knew it had likely played a part in why he was so quick to rush away. They were two strangers thrown together by a foolish kiss almost a year earlier. Now he had returned, it would be difficult to unpick the tangled strands of their lives and find a way to live comfortably with one another, whether that meant together or apart. She could see he was struggling with that, but it didn't mean his leaving so abruptly was painless.

Alice looked at the note again. It was short, only a couple of sentences, informing her he was leaving immediately to travel north and see his family.

'There's nothing wrong with that,' she murmured, trying to convince herself. She took a deep breath and pressed her hands down on the little writing desk, refusing to let this latest development throw her off course.

Loudly she exhaled and stood, pacing back and forth across the room. She had known before they married that she would not have a conventional union. But he had told her that her life would be one way, and now it had completely changed. Of course she was pleased he was not going to die alone, far away from family, but she would like a little acknowledgement that his return affected her as well as him.

With an effort she paused by the window, setting her shoulders and lifting her chin. This was a good lesson to learn. Her husband might be back, but he was not ever going to see her as anything more than the woman he married to save her from ruin. She could not expect affection from or companionship with him, instead she would have to continue as she had been, building a life she was content in, even if she were alone.

Chapter Eleven

The house was quiet as he approached on horseback, each window in darkness despite it being only a little past nine o'clock. This time he had made sure he sent word of his return to London from Northumberland, allowing both his wife and the servants to prepare for his arrival. He wondered if Lady Westcroft had moved from the master bedroom or if she would expect him to sleep elsewhere now she had claimed it as her own this past year. In truth he did not really mind; he'd woken up in many different bedrooms over his lifetime, and another change would not unsettle him. What it did do was highlight one of the many issues they would have to sort out now he had returned to London.

The door opened quickly, and Frank Smith, the young footman, hurried out to hold the reins of his horse to lead it to the back of the house where there was a small stable. Both Simon's father and brother had been keen horsemen, as was he, and his father had added a stable large enough for three horses on the patch of land behind the house. It meant the garden was smaller than it could be, but the horses did not have to be stabled elsewhere whilst he was in residence.

Inside the house was quiet, but Miss Stick came to greet him in the hall and take his hat and gloves.

'Where is Lady Westcroft?' He had spent the journey mentally cataloguing all the issues they needed to discuss now he was back in England, from where they would both live to how they should handle enquiries into their personal lives.

'At the Livingstone ball tonight, my Lord. I doubt she will be back until the early hours of the morning. She tells me it is one of the biggest events of the year, even if half of London has left for their country residences already.'

He frowned. He hadn't considered the possibility his wife would not be at home. He had to admit he had not thought of Lady Westcroft much this past year, but when he had, he'd never thought she would be out enjoying the balls and dinner parties of a London season. Of course he did not begrudge her a little fun, but he was keen to discuss their plans for the future, and after spending the best part of a week on the road to get back to London, he did not want to delay any longer. He'd been a mess when he had left London so abruptly a few weeks earlier, and he regretted fleeing without properly taking his leave of his wife. He wanted to apologise and to begin to discuss the future that they inevitably shared.

'The Livingstone ball?'

'Yes, my Lord. They live just off Grosvenor Square, I believe.'

He checked the time and then nodded decisively. He would go to the ball. Although he had not responded to any invitation, he would not be turned away, and if Lady

Westcroft was there already there would be some expectation that he be in attendance too.

'I need to freshen up and change, then I will go to the ball at the Livingstones' house.'

'Very good, my Lord. We do not have anyone employed as your valet at the moment, but I will send young Smith up with everything you need just as soon as he hands over your horse to the stable-boy.'

'Thank you.'

'You're in the green bedroom,' Miss Stick said, watching him carefully. Many men would refuse to let their wives have the master bedroom, but Simon merely nodded his head and made his way up the stairs.

Ninety minutes later he was standing on the threshold of Mr and Mrs Livingstone's house, wondering if he had made a terrible mistake. Mr Livingstone was obscenely wealthy, having made his money in importing luxury fabrics. It was said even Queen Charlotte waited excitedly for Mr Livingstone's shipments to arrive at the docks and would get first refusal on anything new and exotic. The house was illuminated by hundreds of candles, and even from the doorstep he could hear the loud hum of conversation over the music. If he stepped into the ballroom he would be seen by half the *ton* within seconds, and news of his second return to London would spread quickly.

After a moment he pushed aside the doubts, telling himself he had to return to society at some point. Over the next few months he would need to step up and ensure everything for his tenants was running smoothly and see if there was any work that needed doing to his properties, but he would also have to take up his role as earl again in more public ways. In October he would be expected to return to Parliament, and there were always obligations throughout the social season.

The door opened, and he was welcomed into the house. Thankfully the ball was well underway with a dozen couples dancing in the middle of the ballroom whilst everyone else watched from the sides, talking in little huddles.

'Lord Westcroft, we were not expecting you,' Mrs Livingstone said, hurrying over as soon as she spotted him. 'How delightful to have you back in society after your year of travels.'

'It is wonderful to see you again, Mrs Livingstone.' He craned his neck a little, trying to see if he could spot his wife amongst the guests that lined the ballroom.

'You are looking for Lady Westcroft, no doubt,' Mrs Livingstone said with an indulgent smile. 'She is—'

'On the dance floor,' he murmured before she could finish.

For a moment it felt as though time slowed as his eyes followed Lady Westcroft around the ballroom. She stepped gracefully, with none of the hesitation he had felt from her when they had first danced together at the Midsummer's Eve ball. She looked beautiful in a dress of dark green, the material shimmering as she moved, and the skirt swished around her ankles. It complemented her pale skin and red hair to perfection, and Simon could not take his eyes off her.

She smiled then, and he felt a stab of disappointment that it wasn't at him, watching as she dropped her head back and laughed at something her dance partner had said.

He bowed absently to Mrs Livingstone and made his

way through the crowd of people, murmuring greetings as he went. He could not tear his eyes away from his wife, and as the music swelled and then quietened, he was standing at the front of the small crowd at the edge of the dance floor.

At first she did not notice him standing there, but as she turned to face him and her eyes met his, he saw a shadow cross her face. It was momentary, and if he hadn't been watching her so intently he would have missed it, but he felt a sadness that he could be the one to ruin her evening when she otherwise looked as though she were having a wonderful time.

'You're back, my Lord,' she said, excusing herself from her companion.

'I'm back.'

It wouldn't be a complete shock this time. He had ensured he had written before leaving Northumberland and sent the message by fast rider so she would not be taken by surprise at his arrival, but the good conditions on the roads meant he had made fast progress and was in London a couple of days before he was expected.

'Are you well?'

'Yes, thank you. And you?'

She inclined her head, and for the first time he felt regret at how formal their interaction was. It was entirely his fault, he knew that. He'd married a complete stranger and then disappeared for a year. Of course their conversation was going to be stilted and awkward: they barely knew one another.

'How are Maria and the girls? And your mother?' she asked, warmth flaring in her eyes.

'They are well. The girls have grown and changed a

lot in a year, but they are happy and healthy and have progressed well with their schooling.'

'Are they still terrorising that poor governess?'

'Miss Pickles? Yes, she threatened to leave, and Maria had me intervene to ask her to stay. She doesn't think she'll last more than another month.'

Lady Westcroft smiled indulgently, and he marvelled at how she had managed to build a relationship with his family despite not knowing them at all when he had married her. His sister-in-law spoke of his wife so warmly you would have thought they had been best friends their entire lives, and his mother had chided him for not making Lady Westcroft's life easier this past year. It had forced him to acknowledge the guilt he felt at leaving her so soon after their marriage and not even thinking to write to her throughout the year.

'The girls are well-behaved when they are on their own, but when they are all together, they lose the ability to control that naughty streak,' Lady Westcroft said, her voice filled with love. 'Maria spoke of separating them for their lessons if the governess could not cope with all three of them at once. It will be a shame, but perhaps it is the best solution.'

'They put a frog on the poor woman's dinner plate, slipped it in amongst her vegetables when she wasn't looking. Apparently it hopped onto her fork and looked at her.'

'Was that the event that pushed her towards threatening to leave?'

'One of many, I think,' Simon said. He felt himself begin to relax and was reminded again of how reasonable Lady Westcroft was. It boded well for their marriage of convenience, and he hoped they would be able to come to some arrangement about how to live that would suit both of them.

The music started again, the musicians returned from their short break, refreshments in hand, and Simon recognised a waltz, the music they had danced to on the terrace of the Midsummer's Eve ball almost a year ago.

Without thinking he held out his hand. 'Would you care to dance?'

For a second he saw a flicker of hesitation in her eyes, and then she nodded.

'It would be my pleasure.'

Simon felt the eyes of the room on them as they took their place on the dance floor.

'Why does it feel like everyone is watching us?' Lady Westcroft said, leaning in close to whisper in his ear.

'They are. We haven't been seen in public together before, and no one can work out the truth of our marriage. I am sure they are fascinated by it and want to see if they can pick up any clues as to whether we despise each other or can't keep our hands from one another.'

She smiled then, with a hint of sadness. 'Whereas the truth is much more mundane.'

He placed a hand in the small of her back and adjusted his stance so he was holding her close. It would be a positioning that would be frowned upon at any other time, but they were still considered newly-weds, and there was a certain indulgence for reckless behaviour. As the waltz began he remembered the magic of their first dance together and how she had laughed as she missed a step. He got a sense she was on edge now, but not because she thought she would forget the steps. It was incredible how much she had learned in a year, not least how to fit in at these society events.

'You're grinning,' she whispered.

'I'm remembering our first waltz.'

This made her smile too. 'It was a magical evening.'

'An evening that changed our lives.'

As he twirled her she looked up at him, her face now serious. 'I do appreciate what you did for me. Often I think of what my life would be like married to Cecil.'

'Vile Cousin Cecil,' he said, shaking his head. 'Do you know I had almost forgotten about him.'

'He was outraged when he heard I was going to marry you. He came to my parents' house, stood outside and called me all number of horrible names.'

'I did not realise.'

'My mother counselled me not to tell you. She did not want anything to cause any discord. I think until we were actually standing in front of the vicar she was worried you might change your mind, and she would have two disgraced daughters.' She paused and gave a little shrug of her shoulders even whilst they were dancing. 'I hear from my mother that Cecil is still searching for a wife.'

'I pity the young woman who accepts him.'

'So do I.'

They danced in silence for a minute, and Simon wondered if his wife had taken dance lessons in the time he had been away. She stepped with such confidence now, with the ease of someone who was certain they would not forget the steps. He did not want to insult her by implying she had once not been so graceful and intuitive in her movements, but he was intrigued.

'Please do not take this the wrong way, Lady Westcroft, but you dance beautifully now…' He trailed off as she laughed.

'You mean compared to when we last twirled around a ballroom?'

'I very much enjoyed our dances at the masquerade ball.'

She looked up at him, her expression suddenly serious. 'Your sister-in-law was ever so kind to me after you left. I was like a ship adrift, unsure of what was expected of me or even how to act. She took me in, cocooned me in love, gave me a safe space to grow and discover myself and then urged me to fly once I was ready.'

'Maria is a good woman.'

'The very best,' Lady Westcroft said, strong emotion in her voice. 'When I said I would like to come to London, to look at doing some charitable work and step into society, she ensured I would not make a fool of myself. She taught me how to address people and how to walk into a room with confidence, and we spent many hours twirling round the drawing room, practising dancing, trying not to trip over one of the girls.'

Simon felt a stab of guilt. He should have been the one who guided his new wife through her début in London society; instead, he hadn't even considered it might be somewhere she would want to be.

'I can just imagine it,' he said and to his relief found she was smiling.

'It has been quite the strangest year of my life,' she said quietly, 'but I have learned so much and met so many interesting people.'

'I am glad. Tell me, Lady Westcroft, how did you manage to get these people to accept you?'

'With my rough edges and crude country manners?'

He quickly started to deny that was what he meant and then saw the sparkle of amusement in her eyes.

'You are different to what the ladies of the *ton* are used to.'

'You are not wrong. Did you know when I came to London I got a summons from the palace? The Queen Charlotte herself wanted to cast her eye over me and see what sort of woman you had chosen to be your countess.'

'That cannot have been easy.'

'I almost turned tail and ran all the way back to Northumberland to hide in my childhood bedroom.'

'Yet you stayed. You faced the queen and claimed your place in society.'

'I think her approval helped me greatly. Once she had declared me a darling of the *ton*, everyone wanted to get to know the surprise countess.' She gave a little shake of her head as if remembering the day she had been called to the palace. 'That is not to say that I was confident when I was led down the long corridors to meet the queen. My knees actually knocked together whilst I waited outside to be summoned into her presence.'

'She is a formidable lady,' Simon murmured. 'I am impressed, Lady Westcroft.'

His wife pulled a face and leaned in closer, allowing him to catch a hint of an alluring scent, a mixture of lavender and something else he couldn't quite put his finger on.

'I know there is a great expectation that we address one another formally, but at least in private might you call me Alice? There are three Lady Westcrofts in your family at present, and it gets a little tedious for ever trying to work out who everyone is referring to.'

'Alice,' he said, pleased to be rid of the formality. 'And you should call me Simon.'

'Thank you.'

The music swelled and died away, and they came to a stop in the middle of the dance floor. He bowed and she curtsied, and for a long moment he stared into her eyes. There was something mesmerising about the blue of her eyes, and the spell was only broken when she looked away. He had been going to suggest they take a little refreshment together, perhaps step out of the ballroom into one of the quieter areas so they could spend a little bit of the evening talking, but Alice touched his arm fleetingly and then excused herself, murmuring something about a full dance-card. She disappeared into the press of people around the perimeter of the ballroom before he could protest, leaving him standing alone.

Alice was pleased with the fast pace of the next three dances. It meant she was out of breath towards the end, but also none of her partners expected more than minor snippets of conversation in between the bursts of vigorous footwork. Her partners were all pleasant gentlemen who she had danced with before, mainly husbands of the women she knew socially or through the London Ladies' Benevolent Society.

Out of the corner of her eye she could see her husband prowling around the room. It had been quite a surprise, his turning up this evening. She had expected him back in London in the next few days but had thought they would meet behind closed doors at the townhouse, not at the Livingstones' ball in front of everyone.

After they had shared a waltz, Alice had been eager to get away, hoping that if she kept herself busy and unavailable, her husband might decide to go home or, at the very least, retire to the card tables. Instead he'd watched her constantly, brushing away the attempts by other guests at engaging him in conversation. It was unnerving, and she was sure people were beginning to notice.

She wondered if she could slip away. A carriage waited somewhere outside to take her home once the evening had concluded, but the way Simon was watching her, he would follow her out and suggest they share the carriage home. He was eager to talk, to discuss their future, she could tell by the nervous energy about him, but she needed a little time to compose herself first.

He caught her eye for a second, and she felt a spark travel through her before she quickly looked away. *This* was the problem. Simon had returned to London eager to work out how they would live their lives married but very much separate. It was what she wanted too, to continue to build the success of her charitable work, to find her place in society and enjoy her life in a way she had never been allowed to before this past year. Yet when he stepped close to her, when he looked at her with those brilliant blue eyes, all she could think of was kissing him. It was as if she were swept back to the Midsummer's Eve ball all over again and they were recklessly running through the garden hand in hand. Whenever he came close she felt her heart hammer in her chest, and she got an overwhelming urge to kiss him.

It was highly inconvenient for many reasons, not least because he clearly didn't think of her as anything more than a relative he was responsible for, someone a little troublesome who had been foisted upon him.

She broke eye contact, quickly looking away and trying to work out if there was a way to escape without him seeing her. She hesitated for just a moment too long, and as she stepped away from the dance floor her husband was at her side.

'I do not think there is any more dancing for a while,' he said.

'That is a shame,' she murmured and caught his raised eyebrow. She had to remind herself her husband was an intelligent man and probably had worked out she was trying to avoid him.

'Perhaps we can find somewhere quieter to talk, even if just for a few minutes.'

Alice sighed and then nodded. 'I am fatigued. Unless you wish to stay, shall we share a carriage home?'

He looked relieved, and Alice realised with surprise that he wasn't used to society events. Although he hadn't written to her over the last year, he had sent a couple of short notes to Maria and his mother, and they had shared a little of what his life had been like. From what she could gather he had lived quietly, opting for a villa in a rural location with his closest neighbours some miles away. He had not looked to socialise in his new community, and although his journey back to England would have involved travelling by ship with others, he would not have encountered a situation like this for a long time. Even if he had been attending balls and social gatherings since early adulthood, it would still be quite an adjustment for him to make from his recent experiences.

She felt a little guilty for avoiding him for so long. There were many things he could have done better in their relationship, but wanting to discuss the practicalities of their arrangement now wasn't one of them.

'Should we say goodnight to Mr and Mrs Livingstone?' Alice said as he led her rapidly towards the door.

Simon leaned in, and Alice felt herself shiver as his breath tickled her ear. 'They will not mind if we slip away. They will tell themselves it is only to be expected when two newly-weds are reunited after time apart.'

He placed a hand on the small of her back to guide her, and Alice had to suppress a little groan of frustration. He seemed entirely unaffected by her: it was as if to him the kiss on Midsummer's Eve had never happened.

It took a few minutes to find their carriage amongst the dozens standing outside. Theirs was tucked down a side street, and the driver was sitting on top enjoying the evening air as they approached.

Alice remained silent once they had climbed inside, and Simon instructed the driver to take them home.

It was dark in the carriage as they sat across from one another. Alice could only see the contours of her husband's face and the glint of his eyes in the moonlight, but nothing to help her anticipate how the conversation would begin.

'You looked happy tonight,' Simon said after a minute. 'It was lovely to see.'

His words were not what she expected, and it took her a moment to compose herself enough to answer. 'I am happy,' she said eventually.

'Are you? I worried quite a lot before we married that you were choosing an option that would not give you the life you wanted. You were stuck between a marriage to Cecil and a life that was not the future you had once imagined.'

She was touched that he had considered her feelings in such depth when he'd had so much else to occupy his mind. She chose her words carefully now, not wanting to give him the wrong impression.

'This isn't the life I imagined or the life I hoped for when I was a young girl, yet these last few months I have been content. I cannot lie to you and say I do not sometimes wish for children, for a husband who loves me and a house filled with family, but I am slowly learning there are other ways to seek contentment in life.'

'You are refreshing, Alice,' Simon said, his voice low and serious, a note of wonder about it. 'You always speak your mind even if it makes you vulnerable.'

'I do not think there is any point in lying about one's feelings. If I told you I was blissfully happy and never thought of a different life, then it might influence what we decide on for our future. It is important you know how I really feel. This past year I have not had anyone to hide behind. I've had to assert my own views, to make decisions and bear the consequences.'

'I am sorry you have been so alone.'

'It has not been entirely a bad thing,' she said quietly. 'I have learned a lot about myself and how much more capable I am than I ever realised.'

'I suppose you never had the chance to step out into the world alone before. Young gentlemen often have that taste of independence when they leave home to attend university or go to seek their fortune through work or the military. Yet young women stay under their father's control until they marry.'

'I will always be grateful for the past year. It has shown me I can achieve so much more than I ever thought.'

They fell silent for a moment, and Alice glanced out of the window to see they were already slowing to a stop in front of the townhouse. Their conversation hadn't delved very deep, and she knew soon they would have to sit down across a table from one another and decide what their lives would look like.

Simon helped her from the carriage, and they walked arm-in-arm up the steps to the front door. She felt torn, simultaneously wanting to rip herself away from Simon so he wouldn't have a chance to hurt her and strike up a conversation so he would have to linger.

In the end she bid him goodnight in the hallway and hurried upstairs, feeling her heart pound in her chest as Simon called after her.

'Tomorrow we should talk properly,' Simon said, his voice quiet but clear. She nodded, hoping she would sleep well before the negotiation for her future began.

Chapter Twelve

'Your note was a little cryptic,' Alice said as she strolled into the park, parasol in hand to shield her from the warmth of the sun.

He had been up early, unable to settle. Throughout the night he had been plagued by indecision and by thoughts of his wife that were not helpful in assisting him to come to a sensible conclusion about how he wanted their future to look. He'd risen early and, when there had been no sign of Alice at an early breakfast, had decided to leave her a note to meet him in Hyde Park, dressed in her riding habit.

When he had first arrived in the park it had been quiet, with only a few other early-risers out for a brisk morning walk or for a ride. On his trip back to Northumberland he had picked up his beautiful horse, Socrates, and this morning had enjoyed a long ride without the pressures of travelling on the dusty roads. Before Alice's arrival he had also hired a horse for her to ride. There was something about having the breeze on your face and the thought of freedom to gallop off towards the horizon that helped to clear the mind. It would also ensure their conversation didn't become too heated or

intense. Alice was an immensely pragmatic woman—
he had seen that in how she had reacted to impossible
situations this past year—but they were talking about
her entire future.

He saw her eye with uncertainty the horses he was
holding by the reins.

'You wish for us to ride?'

'I find I do my best thinking on horseback.' He paused
as she regarded the horses with trepidation, realising he
did not even know if his wife could ride. 'You have ridden before?'

She nodded slowly. 'Twice. Both unmitigated disas-
ters.' For a long moment she would not meet his eye,
and then she sighed. 'But I suppose I could try again.'

'What went wrong before?'

'Do you remember my friend Lydia?'

'The young lady you sneaked into the Midsummer's
Eve ball with?'

'Yes. When we were younger she persuaded me to
ride her father's horse with her. We thought it would
be easy, but as soon as we were seated the horse got
spooked and reared up, and Lydia tumbled to the ground.
The horse took off along the high street, and I could do
nothing but close my eyes, cling onto its neck and hope
I did not die.'

'How old were you?'

'Eight or nine. The horse ran for three miles before
it calmed.'

'You managed to stay on its back?'

'Somehow I did.'

'That is impressive.'

'I thought I would die if I fell. We got into so much

trouble I wasn't allowed to see Lydia for a month, and my father took a cane to my hands, whipping them so badly they bled.' She turned over her hands and looked down at them. Simon had the urge to reach out and run his fingers over the skin of her palms but stopped himself just in time.

'What about the second time?'

'That was a little less dramatic, and less illicit. My sister had a suitor in the days before—' She glanced up at him quickly.

Alice had told him of her sister's near disgrace, the weeks of turmoil as the whole family thought there was no way to save Margaret's reputation. Then a surprise proposal had materialised, followed by a quick marriage.

'Before her marriage,' he finished diplomatically.

'Yes. They would go walking over the fields, and I used to have to accompany them to chaperon. One day he brought his horse and suggested I ride. I was nervous, but Margaret was keen as it would give her a little more privacy with this man she thought she might want to marry. I agreed reluctantly, and after I got over my nerves it was quite a pleasant experience, riding through the fields in the sunshine.'

'Did something happen?'

'There was a man out with his dog. The dog got excited and spooked the horse. The horse ran, and at first I managed to hang on, but the path took us under a low hanging branch, and I did not duck in time.'

'That must have hurt.'

'I was lucky I was not seriously injured.'

'I did not know,' Simon murmured quietly, frowning. There was so much he did not know about his wife.

All these little stories from her childhood, her likes and dislikes. It wasn't surprising as he had spent no time with her, but despite his plan to keep a good amount of distance between them, he felt a flicker of sadness. His brother, Robert, had shared everything with Maria, and over the course of their marriage they had learned all those little stories, all the childhood anecdotes that build to mould a person into their adult form. 'We can walk if you prefer.'

Alice inhaled deeply and then shook her head. 'No, I wish to be able to ride. A sedate half an hour around Hyde Park will be a good way to get me over my fear.'

'Only if you are sure.'

She nodded and approached the smaller of the two horses, a docile mare that regarded her with hooded eyes. She took her time, stroking the horse's nose and then neck, talking softly to the animal. Alice might not have ridden for a long time, but she knew how to approach an animal to ensure the encounter was a calm one.

After a few minutes she looked around. 'I am not sure I am strong enough to pull myself onto her back.'

'I will help you.' He looped Socrates's reins over a fence-post and came up behind Alice, guiding her hands to the correct spot on her horse's back to help her to pull herself up. 'Put a foot in my hand, and I will lift you. Once you are high enough, you need to twist around and find a comfortable position in the saddle.'

As he moved closer he caught a hint of her scent and had to resist the urge to lean in farther. It was tantalising, a subtle mix of lavender and rosewater, and he had the sudden desire to press his lips against the soft skin of her neck. There was a spot just behind and below her ear that looked perfect for his lips, and he had to stop himself quickly as he realised he had almost leaned in to kiss it.

His body brushed against hers as she lifted her foot into his hand, and he quickly boosted her into the air. With his help she twisted lithely and was quickly seated in the saddle. He took a minute to help her position her feet and showed her how best to hold the reins, all while trying to ignore the urge to pull her out of the saddle and back into his arms.

He tried to reason it was only natural, this attraction he felt. He had been starved of companionship for a long time, and Alice was an attractive young woman. Never before had he dallied with a respectable unmarried woman, but on the night of the Midsummer's Eve ball nearly a year earlier, he had been unable to resist kissing her, even though he'd known better. That attraction, that deep desire, had not faded in the time he was away, although now it was even more imperative that he did not do anything to jeopardize the delicate balance of their relationship.

Once Alice was settled he pulled himself away and mounted his horse, glancing over to check his wife was not looking too nervous.

'Shall we start with a gentle walk down to the Serpentine?'

'That would be pleasant.'

He urged Socrates on gently and was pleased to see Alice doing the same to her horse, and after a minute he was able to fall into step beside her. They had to wind along a couple of tree-lined paths to get to the wide-open space of the more central area of Hyde Park, but before long they were side by side, riding towards the water.

'How are you finding it?'

'I am a little nervous,' Alice confessed with a self-deprecating smile, 'but I think I am beginning to enjoy it.'

'I am glad. We can stop at any time.'

They rode in silence for a few minutes, and each time he glanced across at Alice he could see she was deep in thought. He realised he knew so little of her hopes and her wants that he had no idea what she would be amenable to when they discussed their future. It was clear she understood they would not have a conventional marriage, even now that he had returned to England, yet it was hard to fathom whether she wished to continue her life completely separate from his or if she wanted companionship from him.

As they approached the sparkling blue water, he slowed and her horse followed his lead, and for a moment they took in the view without saying anything. It was a glorious day, and the park was wonderfully empty despite the pleasant weather.

'Is there somewhere we can go that is a little more private?' Alice said, leaning towards him slightly. 'I do not wish what we discuss to become gossip by this afternoon.'

'Of course. The park is vast. If you are happy to continue with our ride, we can find somewhere we will not be overheard.'

'Thank you.'

He led them away from the lake, pleased to see with every passing minute Alice's confidence was growing, the reins now held loosely in her hands as they allowed the horses to pick the pace. After ten minutes they were away from the people strolling by the water, and it felt as though they had this part of the park to themselves.

As he watched, Alice straightened in her seat as if gearing herself up for battle. He felt a stab of regret that they needed to have this discussion but also knew that once their expectations and preferences were out in the open, they could move away from the uncertainty that surrounded them both.

'You wished to discuss our future, Simon,' Alice said, glancing over at him but not holding his eye. He could sense her trepidation of the subject but was pleased she had initiated the conversation.

'I think we both need to know where we stand.'

'Do you wish to divorce me?' she said, her voice low. Simon was an experienced rider, but in his shock he almost fell out of his saddle.

'Divorce you? Whatever gave you that idea?'

She looked at him incredulously for almost a minute before replying. 'You married me thinking you would be dead within a few months, so that our union was an act of duty that would not really affect you. Now that you have been told you are not imminently going to be struck down, in fact you may never be in the way your brother and your father were, I expect you wish to return to your normal life to a certain degree.'

'I am not going to divorce you, Alice. That would ruin us both.'

'I would not try to stop you,' she said softly.

'Do you want me to divorce you?' he asked, unable to fathom how divorce had even entered her mind. Divorce was a messy and protracted affair, and he had only seen it occur a couple of times, and on each occasion neither party had come out unscathed. He found he was upset at even the idea of divorcing Alice.

'No,' she said quickly. 'Far from it. From the whispered conversations I have heard about when Lord Southerhay divorced his wife eight years ago, I can see it is a catastrophic course of events with both parties completely humiliated by the discussion of their private business in front of Parliament itself. I am aware if you divorced me my life as I know it would be over. I doubt I would ever marry again, and I wouldn't have children, a family. My own family would disown me. It would be the worst possible outcome.' She paused and then looked over at him, holding his eye. 'But I do understand if that is the path you wish to take. I am not what you had planned for your life, and if you now want to find a wife you actually want to marry, I will understand.'

'I am not that heartless, Alice,' he said, his voice low. He felt a flicker of anger that she would think so little of him and had to remind himself she had only known neglect and desertion from him. Divorce was a fate worse than death to many and happened only once in a generation in their social class. Yet surely she would understand they had entered into this marriage to save her from ruin, and he wouldn't callously abandon her now.

'Not divorce, then,' she said, nodding with relief.

'Not divorce, we can agree on that.' He paused, wondering how he was going to say what he had to. Despite not knowing Alice well, he did know she wanted a family one day. She had spoken of being surrounded by children, of a happy family life with a husband who loved her. He remembered how she had been with the two children in Hyde Park, sailing the model boat on the

Serpentine. At that image he felt the words stick in his throat. That was not the life he could give her.

'I may have been told by the doctors the headaches were not a harbinger of imminent death, but I still cannot know what the future might hold,' he said slowly, watching Alice's reaction. 'I may suffer the same fate as my father and my brother, and it could happen at any time. It has meant addressing my mortality each and every day, knowing this could be my last. I was eager to return to England to see my family and to take up my responsibilities once again, but it does not change the fact that one day in a few months or years I may have to leave suddenly again, or I may die without any warning.'

'That could be said for any of us,' Alice said softly. 'I do not mean to take away from the seriousness of your situation—of course your risk is greater—but none of us know what the future will hold. I may catch consumption from one of the children at the orphanage tomorrow and wither away within the next six months, or I could be thrown from this horse and crack my skull this afternoon.'

'You are not wrong. I know it is foolish to live one's life always thinking about whether today is the day you die, but I find it is not a thought I can change just by intention.'

Alice nodded slowly. 'I understand that,' she said, giving him a sad smile. 'Although, I wish it were not so.'

'It also means that I will not have children. I refuse to bring a child into this world who might suffer the same.'

He could see Alice had more to say, perhaps more to argue on this subject, but after a moment she pressed her lips together and nodded. 'I understand,' she said simply.

Looking at her intently he spoke a little softer. 'I know this is not the life I promised you. I offered a year or two of comfort with your reputation intact, and then perhaps a few months of mourning before you could start looking for a husband of your own choice. A man you wanted to marry and who would give you your family.'

Alice looked away, but before she did, he thought he saw tears in her eyes. He felt like a cad, ripping away her hopes for the future like this.

'I do not begrudge you being alive, Simon,' she said softly. 'Whatever that means for my future.'

They were kind words from a kind young woman, and for a moment he wanted to pull her into his arms, hold her close to him and tell her he would give her whatever she wanted, yet he couldn't do it. Their lives were destined to go in very different directions, and as much as he liked Alice, as much as he desired her and could see himself being happy with her if they lived a conventional life as husband and wife, it wasn't a path he could take.

He couldn't bring himself to voice the other reason he couldn't build a true relationship with her—it was buried too deep inside and he didn't like to examine it too closely—but there was a part of him that felt as though he were stealing his brother's life. He had the title, the properties, the place in Parliament, all the things his brother should be enjoying still. If he allowed himself to have a normal life with Alice, to treat her as his true wife, to have children with her, that would be a step too far in assuming the life that should have been his brother's.

Alice took a deep breath and seemed to brace herself for what she had to say next.

'I understand you do not want to have children, that you are concerned about passing to them whatever it is your father and brother were afflicted by. I also understand that means we cannot have an intimate relationship as is normal between husband and wife.'

He hadn't expected she would be so direct, but he was pleased that there was no ambiguity in her words. The last thing they wanted was to speak in metaphors and then both leave with a different understanding of what the future would hold.

'I am not sure what it is you do want, Simon. Do you wish for us to lead completely separate lives? For me to reside in Northumberland whilst you are in London, and then when you travel north we cross on the road when I am heading for London? Or do you want us to have a closer relationship, a friendship, a companionship? It is very hard to know what to suggest when I have no idea what it is you would be comfortable with.'

Up until he had arrived back in England, he would have said the first of her suggestions was the one that made the most sense, but now, even after spending just a few scattered hours with Alice, he wasn't sure he wanted to move around the country like ships passing in the night, barely acknowledging she existed. Whilst he was in Italy, his marriage had seemed an abstract concept, something that was very easy to put out of his mind, but now that he had returned it was far harder to ignore her, and he realised he didn't wish to.

'I propose a friendship, perhaps with time, even a companionship. We do not need to be tied to one another, if you wish to stay in London when I go to Northumberland, then there is no issue. If I wish to visit friends, then I will inform you, but there is no expectation that we conduct every aspect of our lives together.'

'That sounds agreeable,' Alice said. 'So we shall endeavour to at least keep the other person informed of our plans.'

'Yes,' he murmured. 'I know I left rather abruptly a few weeks ago when I travelled to Northumberland. I should have informed you in person. I was overwhelmed by my return home, but it is no excuse for leaving without bidding you farewell. I am sorry.'

'Thank you.'

They had ridden some way across the open grass now and were in a deserted part of the park. There was a good view over the green space up here, and for a moment Simon paused to take it all in. He felt a roil of emotion as he let his eyes take in the rooftops of London beyond the park. When he'd left England eleven months ago, he had thought he would never look upon this view, nor see his beloved Northumberland again either. His homecoming had proved more emotional than he had imagined.

'I have brought some refreshment. Shall we pause here and toast our marriage with a glass of lemonade?'

'That sounds lovely.' Alice smiled at him, and for an instant he had the urge to throw away every caution and pull her into his arms, to hell with the consequences. Quickly he pushed the thought away: he had given in to his desire once with Alice, and that had upended both their lives. He must control himself better around his pretty wife.

Chapter Thirteen

Alice tried to push away the desire she felt as Simon wrapped his hands around her waist to help her from her saddle. It was an impossible situation, and she had to do everything in her power not to make it worse.

She considered his offer of friendship, companionship perhaps, and realised it was better than she had feared but not what she had secretly hoped for. It was ridiculous to even think about, but deep down she knew she wished Simon had come racing back to London because he had suddenly realised he could not live without her. It was so far from the truth of the matter it was almost laughable. He did not want to live with her as most men wanted to live with their wives. He would treat her as a spinster relative, with kindness and perhaps even a little platonic affection, but there would be no intimacy, no love.

Alice pushed away the disappointment. This way was better. She could continue with her life here in London, travel to Northumberland to see Maria and the children as planned later in the summer, take her trips to visit her own sister. Sometimes Simon would be at home when she returned, sometimes he would not. Her life would not change substantially, and perhaps with a little time she would grow to enjoy this new phase.

She was determined not to become reliant on Simon's company, though. He had shown how quickly he could disappear and how little importance he placed on including her in his plans. She would have to conduct her life with this in mind, always wary that he could disappear at any moment.

With his hands around her waist, Simon steadied Alice as she slid to the ground. They ended up standing close, and Alice could not resist the urge to raise a hand and place it on his chest. Even through the layers of clothing, she could feel his heart beating, slow and steady underneath the subtle rise and fall as he inhaled and exhaled. She glanced up at him and saw him regarding her strangely, with an almost hungry look in his eyes, and she realised that desire for her he had shown on the night of the Midsummer's Eve ball had not disappeared completely. He was holding himself tight, coiled like a deadly snake ready to spring out at its prey, and she realised with a rush of satisfaction she was making him feel on edge.

She was pleased not at his discomfort but that she was not the only one struggling to deny she felt something more than a desire for friendship between them.

Alice allowed her hand to linger for another few seconds and then withdrew, stepping to the side to move around him, trying to pretend nothing had happened. Despite being a married woman of eleven months, she was still very much an innocent in the ways of seduction. However, people assumed she had at least had her wedding night with her husband, and it meant she was no longer shielded from some of the more delicate conversations held between married women.

She had no plans to try to seduce Simon: not only would she have no idea how to go about it but also it wouldn't be fair. She might not agree with his reasons for deciding not to have children, but it *was* his decision, and she would not trick him into any intimacy in the hopes that she might have the family she dreamed of. Instead she would work on making the life she did have as fulfilling as possible, and perhaps dreaming of her husband's lips on hers last thing at night when they went to bed.

Simon lingered by the horses for a moment and when he turned to face her, he looked composed with no hint of the desire that had flashed in his eyes when she'd stood close.

He took a blanket from the saddlebag on his horse and spread it on the grass, indicating for her to have a seat. She lowered herself to the ground, making herself comfortable on the soft wool of the blanket. From the saddlebag he also produced a large bottle of lemonade and a parcel that she suspected contained some of Cook's delicious biscuits.

He brought them over, indicating the lemonade. 'I forgot glasses,' he said with a shrug. 'We will have to drink from the bottle.'

'I do not mind. When I was young my parents would sometimes take us for picnics on the beach in the summer when it was a particularly hot day. We would walk across the dunes and find a quiet spot, spread out a blanket and enjoy our lunch with the sea lapping at the shore in the distance. My mother never remembered to pack glasses, and Margaret and I always shared lemonade straight from the bottle.'

'It sounds idyllic.'

Alice wobbled her head from side to side. She couldn't complain about her childhood, not when she compared it to the awful circumstances the children in the London orphanages and on the streets lived in, yet it had not been happy. There had been happy times, long summer days spent playing with Lydia and her sister, paddling in the sea and coming home soaked through with seawater, the winter storms where she and Margaret would creep to the empty attic room and watch the thunder and lightning light up the village and the sand dunes beyond. She had some fond memories, but there had always been an uneasiness in their house. Her father was strict, even more so than most parents she knew. He would bring out his cane if he thought she or Margaret had committed any more substantial infractions of his rules. Often the girls would be unable to eat their dinner because their punishment had split the skin on their hands.

Their mother had not been so coldly cruel, but she had expected quiet obedience from her two daughters and was quick to anger if they did not obey. It had not been a happy childhood, but she had been clothed and housed in comfort, with decent meals on the table.

'You have happy memories?'

'I used to enjoy the times I had playing on the beach with my sister,' Alice said, deciding not to mention the difficult feelings she had towards her parents.

'That is a well-practised answer. You are skilled at diplomacy, Alice.' He regarded her as he sat down. 'Am I to take it your childhood wasn't idyllic?'

She puffed her cheeks out and then blew out the air before shaking her head.

'It wasn't idyllic,' she said slowly. 'It wasn't terrible, but my parents were distant and cold, and I was always one step away from punishment. I cannot complain when I see what some children have to endure, but it is not the way I would want to bring my children up.' She glanced at him quickly before adding, 'If ever I have them.'

'It is perhaps why you are so interested in the work with children on the streets and in orphanages that the London Ladies' Benevolent Society does.'

'I think you may be right,' she said, taking the bottle of lemonade after he had popped out the cork for her. It felt strange to swig from a bottle in front of this man she barely knew, but she was thirsty, and after a moment she pushed away her reticence and took a delicate sip. The lemonade was delicious and refreshing, and she decided to forget about what she looked like or what Simon thought of her and took a long gulp of the beverage. 'Since I have taken over the helm I have steered the society towards projects that help women and children. We do a lot of fundraising and donate to many good causes, but there has been a definite shift to help the most vulnerable in society with our efforts.'

'I have been making enquiries,' Simon said as he sat beside her. The blanket wasn't huge, and he sat close without his position being scandalous. They were a married couple and there was nothing wrong with them sharing some refreshment whilst seated together in a public park, yet somehow when his hand brushed hers it felt as though they were doing something illicit.

'Enquiries?'

'Into your society. I am impressed. What you have managed to do in a year is nothing short of extraordinary.'

A subtle warmth diffused through her body, making her skin tingle at his compliment.

'It has taken up much of my time these last few months, but I feel like we are finally making a difference where it is most needed.'

She glanced at him and decided she would share a little more. He looked engaged and interested, and although she had vowed she would continue her life in the knowledge he might leave it at any moment, she did not have to petulantly shut him out of her world.

'Lady Kennington has identified a small orphanage close to the slums of St Giles that she thinks would benefit immensely from our patronage. Apparently it is a dilapidated building that takes from the poorest areas. I am planning on visiting later today to see whether we will be able to help.'

'I am sure any donations will be thankfully received.'

'I hope we might be able to offer more than that. Many of the ladies from the Benevolent Society are keen to do more than just fundraise. We have a mix of backgrounds and a wealth of expertise at our disposal. It will depend on who runs the orphanage, but I am hopeful we might be able to provide more than just money.'

'What do you mean?' He leaned forward, looking intrigued, and Alice felt a rush of satisfaction at his interest.

'One of the main limitations of many of the orphanages is the lack of support as the children get to the age when they are no longer eligible for a bed and a hot meal from the establishment. They may have rudimentary reading and writing skills, perhaps very basic arithmetic, and they will be trained to do a number of menial household jobs, but often it is not enough. People see they are from the orphanage and will not give them a chance, except in the very lowest paid positions.'

'I cannot argue with the truth of that.'

'I am not sure exactly what the answer is yet. Perhaps better schooling, perhaps a focus on certain trades and skills for when they leave the orphanage. I am hoping with a small establishment like St Benedict's we may be able to foster a system where some of our benefactors look to take in the young boys and girls when they reach fourteen and help to train them as maids and footmen. It may take a little patience, but I believe with the right people it could make the world of difference.'

'A little like your scheme to match the wealthier families with the poorer to provide support over the winter in Bamburgh.'

She felt her cheeks flush, finding that she was pleased he had remembered.

'It is an admirable idea, but it would be a big adjustment, asking these children to abide by the rules of a wealthy and prominent household.'

Alice shook her head vehemently. 'It is the perfect time to do it. They have been used to strict rules for years, being told exactly what they can do and when by the master or matron of the orphanage. It is better to take them from that environment, before there have been too many other corrupting influences.' She cocked her head to one side. 'You have borne witness to this scheme in action.'

He looked at her in surprise. 'I have?'

'Yes, in the young footman, Frank Smith.'

'He is a lad from an orphanage?'

'Yes. I had a long discussion with Miss Stick about whether she would be supportive of the idea of bringing him in to train up.'

'She was happy to do it?'

'Very happy. Miss Stick has a hard demeanour but a very good soul,' Alice said affectionately. 'We visited the orphanage together to talk to Frank and to check he would be a good fit, then he joined the household five months ago.'

'Five months ago he was an orphanage boy?'

'He was.'

Simon let out a low whistle. 'I would not have guessed.'

'Three times a week he spends an hour with either myself or Miss Stick to develop his reading and writing and arithmetic skills, and once he is secure in basic knowledge, we will discuss what he wishes to do with his life and hopefully be able to guide him in that direction.'

'That is an ambitious plan, Alice,' Simon said, looking at her in wonder. 'You think this will work?'

She shrugged. 'I think with Frank it will. He is a determined young man who has seen the worst of life at a very young age, and he is motivated not to end the same way his own parents did, in poverty, unable to support their family. I am not saying it is the answer for everyone, but perhaps it is enough to help a few.'

'Once Frank has gained the skills he needs to get a job elsewhere, you will repeat the process I assume?'

'That is the plan, whilst gently advocating for others to do the same.'

'What if it goes wrong?'

She put her hands a little behind her bottom and leaned back, tilting her face up to the sun underneath the rim of her bonnet. Her skin would burn if she stayed this way for too long, but a couple of minutes would not matter, and it felt so glorious to have the warmth of the sun on her face.

'You mean what if one of the children from the orphanage steals all the silver or brings the household into disrepute?' She shrugged again. 'It is the risk you take when you hire any servant. References can be forged, recommendations coerced. At least this way you know the person's background, and you can learn what they have been through.'

For a minute Simon remained silent, and then he nodded thoughtfully. 'I think the scheme has merit. It will be interesting to see what comes of it.' It was the first time he had spoken of being interested in something shared in the future, and Alice wondered if he would really stick around to see the results of her plans or if in a few months he would disappear again, his only correspondence a short note telling her he was gone.

'I am visiting St Benedict's Orphanage this afternoon. I will keep you updated on my progress.'

Simon frowned. 'I hope you do not plan to go alone. It is not in a salubrious part of the city.'

'I am meeting the matron of the orphanage. I hardly think my life will be in danger.'

'You should take someone with you.'

'Are you volunteering?' It was said in jest, but she saw Simon tilt his head to one side as he considered.

'I am. I have no plans this afternoon. I would be happy to accompany you.'

For a moment she didn't know what to say. Part of her felt unsettled: it was strange enough having her husband back in her life, sharing her home, but she had not expected him to have any involvement with the charity work she did too.

'Thank you,' she said eventually.

'As pleasant as this has been, we should head back home soon,' Simon said, rising to his feet and holding out a hand to help her up. She stood, her body bumping lightly against his, and for a moment she felt as though time stood still. The sensible part of her mind screamed for her to step away, to put some distance between them, but her body just would not obey. She wished she didn't feel this attraction towards her husband. He had made it perfectly clear there would be no intimacy between them, yet she yearned for him to kiss her, to trail his fingers over her skin and make her feel truly alive.

With great effort she stepped away, turning her back for a moment to compose herself. By the time she turned back, Simon had moved and was busying himself with the horses, seemingly unperturbed by their moment of closeness.

Chapter Fourteen

St Benedict's Orphanage was based in a run-down building that had been built on the very edge of the slums of St Giles. It was tucked between two equally rickety buildings, one of which leaned forward over the street as if threatening to collapse any moment. When they had stepped out of the carriage, Simon had looked up and down the street dubiously, wondering how likely it was that the whole row would collapse and crush everyone inside. Such tragedies were not unheard of in these areas where the buildings were poorly constructed in the first place and decades of hard use had chipped away at any structural integrity that might have once been present.

The inside of the orphanage was not much better. There were sloping wooden floors, small windows and a staircase that creaked ominously whenever anyone climbed it. The rooms were dark and draughty, and the accommodation consisted of one long, thin room for the boys and another of similar proportions for the girls. Downstairs there was a communal area set with tables where the orphans both ate and did their lessons.

Despite the grim conditions the children lived in, Simon had been pleasantly surprised when he met Mrs

Phillips, the kindly woman appointed matron of the orphanage by the board of governors. There were twenty-four children under her care, all thin and pale, but neatly turned-out with faces scrubbed and hair cut short to guard against lice.

She had spoken passionately about the work she did in measured tones but with an accent that made Simon think she had grown up locally, perhaps even a child of the slum herself once. She certainly was a good advocate for the orphanage.

They were now sitting at the back of the room whilst the children were finishing their lessons. All twenty-four were taught together, despite them ranging in ages from two to fourteen. They sat, boys on one side of the room, girls on the other, the youngest at the front and the oldest at the back. At the front of the room the teacher pointed to letters and phrases written out, and the children had to read out in unison what they said.

'Look,' Alice whispered, motioning to a few children in the middle of the room. As well as reading the words they were also copying them onto slate tablets. 'I think they only have four slate tablets between twenty-four children.' She shifted a little, leaning forward to see a little better. 'That is something we could easily donate funds for.'

As she sat back, her arm brushed against his, a fleeting contact, but it made him stiffen all the same. He realised he liked this version of his wife. Here at the orphanage, the naïve country girl he had married was long gone; instead, there was an idealistic woman who was determined to make a difference in the world. When she conversed with the matron, she spoke with conviction and confidence, a woman who was used to being listened to.

After a few more minutes the lessons finished and the children filed out of the classroom, some into the kitchen beyond to get started on helping to prepare the evening meal, others upstairs where no doubt some other work waited for them. They moved quietly, a little subdued, and Simon felt a pang of pity for those who had lost their families and now lived in this dull, monotonous life, although he supposed it was better than the alternative that waited for them on the streets.

'Thank you for your visit, Lady Westcroft,' Mrs Phillips said as she ushered the last of the children upstairs and came to stand with them. 'We are most honoured in your interest in our small orphanage.'

'I am grateful for your hospitality and your honesty,' Alice said warmly. Mrs Phillips had a positive outlook, but she had not glossed over the shortcomings of the small orphanage, letting them see the bad alongside the good. 'We have our next meeting of the London Ladies' Benevolent Society in two weeks. I will report back to our members, and I am hopeful we will be able to offer some monetary and practical support.' Alice paused, looking at the matron with an assessing gaze, then nodded as if making a decision. 'I am conscious of your years of experience, Mrs Phillips, and I am wary of charging in and suggesting changes that may not be helpful, despite our best intentions. I wonder if you might take some time to write down what you think might be helpful so I can present your thoughts to the other members, or consider if you were willing to even come and talk to the ladies yourself.' Alice held up her hands and smiled at the matron. 'I know you are terribly busy, but give it some thought, and let me know what you can manage.'

'I will, Lady Westcroft.' Mrs Phillips turned to Simon. 'It is a pleasure to meet you, Lord Westcroft.'

'And you, Mrs Phillips.' He inclined his head and then offered Alice his arm as the matron showed them out.

Their carriage was waiting outside, surrounded by a gaggle of curious children. Simon was about to gently shoo them away when Alice gripped his arm.

'Thank you,' she said, looking up at him with her pale blue eyes. She had a contented smile on her face, and Simon felt a desire to keep that smile on her lips for ever.

'What for?'

'I admit I have only had the one husband,' she said with a mischievous glance at him, 'and that husband only for a few days, but I have seen how other men treat their wives. They disregard their views, silence their opinions. Many other men would have insisted on taking the lead with Mrs Phillips, even if it were not their cause to lead on. You did not. You stepped back and allowed me to be the one to ask questions and be in control, even for that short amount of time.'

'Most men are fools,' he murmured. 'They do not listen long enough to their wives to realise what they have to offer the world.' He smiled at her, feeling a unfamiliar satisfaction. This past year he had lived a lonely life, and he realised with a jolt that spending time with Alice, with her kind manner and lively conversation, were just what he needed. Despite the urge he felt to stand on the street corner staring into his wife's eyes, he motioned to the carriage. 'Shall we return home before we become targets for every cutpurse in London?'

Alice inclined her head, but as they stepped from the kerb to cross the road to their carriage, a group of beggar children broke off from the main gaggle and surrounded them, clamouring for money.

There were a couple of older boys in the group, but most of the children were no more than seven. Out of the corner of his eye, Simon saw a man leaning against the wall of a building on the other side of the street, and suddenly he felt a cold chill run through him. The man was resolutely not looking at them despite them being in his direct line of sight. It was suspicious, and without saying anything Simon reached out to grip hold of Alice's arm, wanting to pull her closer to him.

He'd had a privileged upbringing with most of his childhood spent on the estate in Northumberland, but his time travelling had taught him to be vigilant and trust his instincts. He believed the human mind was very good at working out when there was something wrong: it was why people talked of following their gut. Right now his gut was telling him to get his wife out of this situation as quickly as possible.

Alice looked at him in shock as he wrapped an arm around her waist and propelled her through the crowd of children, into the carriage. They had almost made it to the door when one of the younger boys stepped in front of them and with lightning-fast speed whipped out a knife. He held it low so it was hidden from any casual onlooker by the press of bodies around them. Simon saw the boy's hand was shaking, the knife weaving from side to side. He was a pale, scrawny lad, his face grimy and his feet bare on the cobbles. He looked pitiful rather than threatening, and as Simon watched the knife he realised it was likely a distraction. Whilst their eyes were fixed on the blade someone else would be trying to pick his pocket or relieve Alice of anything valuable.

He spun, reaching out to grab the thin wrist of an even younger boy whose hand had slipped inside Simon's jacket. The boy cried out in fear, and after a second the crowd of beggars that surrounded them disappeared, the children scarpering in different directions, diving into alleyways or dashing around corners. Simon looked up, past the carriage, to see the man who had been observing them calmly walking away too.

Only he, Alice and the little pickpocket remained.

The boy struggled, wriggling and tugging at his wrist, desperation on his face as he realised there was no escaping this predicament.

'Stop it,' Simon said, his voice firm but not cruel. The boy looked only five or six, although it was hard to tell as he was clearly malnourished, his growth no doubt stunted by a poor diet.

The boy stilled, looking up at Simon for the first time with big brown eyes.

Next to him he felt Alice shift, but he dared not take his attention from the boy in front of him.

'I don't want to hang,' the boy said after a minute, tears forming in his eyes and rolling onto his cheeks, making tracks through the dirt.

'You're not going to hang,' Simon said, moderating his tone. 'How old are you?'

The boy sniffed. 'Seven.'

Simon grimaced. If he handed this lad to a magistrate

and insisted he be punished for attempting to steal his purse, the child could end up taking a trip to the gallows. Some judges were more lenient towards the younger children that appeared before them, but others looked to set an example to thousands of children who committed crimes each year just looking to fill their hungry bellies.

'What is your name?'

The boy pressed his lips together and shook his head. Alice crouched down, seeming not to notice as the hem of her dress brushed against the dirt of the cobbles.

'What is your name?' she asked this time, her voice soft as if she were talking to one of their nieces.

'Peter, miss.' The boy looked at Alice, and then the tears started to flow from his eyes like a river after a winter storm. 'I don't want to hang, miss. Please don't let him hang me.'

'You're not going to hang,' Simon said firmly. 'There was a man watching us. Tall, dark hair, green coat. Was he with you?'

The boy nodded miserably.

'He told you what to do?'

Again the boy nodded.

'What is his name?'

'I can't tell you. He'll gut me if I do, and that's even worse than hanging.'

'Is he your father?' Alice asked.

'No, my father's dead.'

'What about your mother?'

The boy's eyes darted to the side, and he shrugged.

'Your mother is alive?' Simon said, waiting for the boy to look at him again. He still held the lad by the wrist, knowing as soon as he loosened his grip, the young boy would disappear into the warren of streets that made up St Giles.

Peter nodded glumly.

'Do you live near here?'

Again the boy nodded.

Simon turned to the driver of the carriage who had hopped down from his seat to join them.

'Drummond, take my wife home. Ensure she is escorted safely all the way to the front door.'

Simon turned to Alice to see her frowning.

'You mean to send me back alone?'

'You will be quite safe with Drummond, in the carriage.'

'It is not my safety I fear for.'

He looked at his wife for a moment, realisation dawning. 'You wish to see where this boy lives too?'

'He is only seven, Simon, and clearly he was under the influence of that man who was watching us. I do not want to see him punished.'

'You think I do not mean it when I say I do not want to see him hanged?'

Alice didn't say anything, but her lack of denial hurt more than he thought possible. He might not plan to be a true husband to his wife, but to realise how little she trusted him was difficult to accept.

'I merely want to take this boy home to his family and have a quiet word with his mother. She may be pragmatic, she may not, but I cannot merely let the boy go,' Simon said, his voice low. 'He will be off through the streets and back into the arms of the gang that pressed him to pick my pocket.' He spoke sharply and saw Alice recoil slightly, but she did not retreat.

'I shall come with you, then.'

'Lead the way, Peter,' Simon said brusquely.

Sullenly the young boy led them through a maze of streets to a set of rickety steps that led up to a wooden platform.

'Up there,' Peter said, motioning with his head. The streets were busy and they were drawing curious looks, and Simon found he wanted to get this over with, deliver the boy back to his mother and get Alice home to safety.

They climbed the stairs, and Simon knocked on the door, hearing the sound of a crying baby inside before the murmur of a low voice. After a minute the door opened, and a young woman peered out. She was in her twenties, but already her face was lined and her skin sallow. She held a baby in her arms and was bobbing up and down to soothe it. Her eyes widened as she saw Peter, and she looked up at Simon fearfully.

'What has he done?' she said, her voice cracking.

'You are Peter's mother?'

'Yes. What trouble has he found now?'

'He was in the company of a number of other children and a man who seemed to be directing them to pick people's pockets.'

The woman's face paled, and she reached out for her son, a protective look on her face.

'Don't blame my Peter, please, sir. He's only seven, only a young boy. He's hungry, that's all. We haven't been able to afford much food these last few months, not since his father died. Please don't report him. They'll make an example of him, I know they will.'

To his surprise Alice stepped forward and laid a hand on the woman's arm.

'We are not going to report him. We just wanted to be sure he got home to you safely.'

'And to let you know he is running with a group of pickpockets. If he continues with them, the next time he gets caught, whoever catches him may not be so lenient.'

'You're not going to report him?'

'No.' Simon let go of Peter's wrist, and the boy slipped into the darkness of the room behind his mother, peering out from behind her with a stunned look on his face.

'Thank you, sir. I will make sure he doesn't do anything like this again.'

Simon nodded and then took a step back. There was nothing more they could do here. In all likelihood Peter would be back with the gang of pickpockets first thing tomorrow, choosing to risk his neck rather than endure the relentless hunger he must feel each and every day. It was an awful situation, but now the boy was home safe he had to hand responsibility over to his mother.

He gestured to Alice that they should leave, and she gave Peter's mother one final reassuring smile before they climbed back down the rickety steps.

They walked in silence for a few minutes, navigating the maze of streets until they stepped back out to where the carriage was waiting.

Once inside Simon settled back on his seat and watched the orphanage disappear from view as the carriage rolled away. He was still hurt by Alice's mistrust of him, and he knew he needed to address it lest it eat away at him.

Before he could speak Alice leaned forward and placed her hand on his. It wasn't an overly intimate gesture, at least not for a wife to a husband in normal circumstances, but even the most innocent of touches seemed to ignite something inside him and made it impossible to focus.

'Thank you,' she said, looking across at him and giving him a soft smile.

'You did not trust I would not hand the boy over to a magistrate,' Simon said, watching as Alice stiffened and then nodded slowly.

'You are right,' she said eventually, then let out a deep sigh. 'We do not really know one another at all, do we, Simon?'

'Have I ever done anything to make you think I am an unreasonable man?'

'No,' she said quickly. 'You have always done exactly what you said you would.'

'Then, why doubt me?'

'Do you know how many hours we have spent in one another's company?'

He shook his head.

'Eight. Eight hours. Three at the Midsummer's Eve ball a year ago, one in the weeks before our wedding and one hour after we were married, then three in the days since you have returned. I have spent more time with my hatmaker in the last year, and I absolutely loathe hats.' She was speaking fast now, and he saw the pent-up frustration in her eyes. Their ride through Hyde Park earlier had been pleasant and their discussion reasonable, but he realised much of that was because Alice had been holding back the hurt she was feeling at how he had abandoned her. 'How am I meant to know how you will react to a certain situation? How am I meant to trust your word? We are two strangers tiptoeing around one another, neither sure how the other will react.' She sniffed and turned her head away, blinking furiously. After a moment she turned back. 'I *know* it has to be this way, Simon. I can understand your reasons and I accept them, but it does not mean you can have it both ways. Either you stay distant, living your life without the complication of another's feelings or you allow me close, but if you choose the former you must understand you cannot have the perks without the drawbacks.' She sat back, her chest heaving and her cheeks flushed with colour.

'I thought we had come to an understanding in the park.'

'Friendship?'

'Yes. A decision we would both live our lives independently, but with consideration of the other person.'

She looked at him then, a fierce intensity burning in her eyes, and for a moment he thought he saw a flash of desire, but then she pressed her lips together and inhaled sharply.

'You chide me for not trusting you, yet trust must be built, as must a friendship. I thought that was what you were doing, accompanying me to the orphanage, trying to build some common ground between us, but perhaps I was wrong.'

'You were not wrong, Alice,' he said, sitting back and running a hand through his hair. 'God's blood, I'm trying. This is difficult for me as well.'

She snorted and shook her head, and he felt a swell of anger rise inside him.

'I grant you it is more difficult for you, to have me return alive when I had promised you your freedom, but I too am trying to navigate an impossible situation.'

She leaned forward, jabbing a finger in his direction. 'Do not imply I want you dead.'

'It would be far simpler for you if I were.'

'You think I am that cruel?'

Simon felt the momentary anger simmer and then die away inside him, and he lowered his voice.

'No,' he said quietly. 'Of course not. Forgive me, that was unacceptable.'

Alice looked at him, her eyes narrowed. 'Just because you do not think you deserve to be alive doesn't mean I would ever agree with you. I went into this marriage with my eyes open, and although it may not be exactly what you promised, I would never, ever wish you were dead so that I could have my freedom.' She paused to draw in a ragged breath. '*You* are not a victim here, Simon. You get to dictate how our lives continue. You have the position of power. You say we cannot have a normal marriage,' she said and snapped her fingers, 'so we do not have a normal marriage. You say we cannot have children—' another snap of the fingers '—no children. You say we will work towards a friendship.' The third snap seemed to pierce his very soul. 'Friendship it is.'

Her words cut through him, and he gripped the seat, trying to anchor himself as the world spun around him.

For a long time they were silent, and the carriage was travelling through familiar streets before Simon was able to speak again.

'What do you mean, I do not think I deserve to be alive?'

'It is true, is it not?'

He shook his head, but even to him the movement was unconvincing.

'When you left, your mother and your sister-in-law

were devastated. It was as though they were in mourning, and for two women who had lost so much already, it nearly broke them.'

Simon closed his eyes for a moment, knowing this was going to be hard to hear. He had known his departure to Italy would be painful for those who loved him, but at the time he had thought it would ultimately protect them.

'Your mother couldn't get out of bed for a week.' She held up a hand. 'I do not tell you this to punish you, to make you feel guilty, but I think it is important you realise the impact of your actions on those who love you.'

'I knew it would be hard for them, but I thought it better than the alternative.'

'When your mother was up to having visitors, I went and sat with her every day, and she told me all about you and your family. She told me of how you idolised your father, how he was a wonderful man who both you and your brother looked up to. She told me of how his death had ripped you apart. A boy of twelve needs his father, and you lost yours in one of the worst ways imaginable.'

The carriage was beginning to slow as they approached the house, but Simon knocked loudly on the roof and stuck his head out the window, telling the driver to loop around until he was instructed otherwise.

'You mourned him deeply, but you still had your brother. Your mother told me you loved Robert more than anyone else.'

'He was the best of men.'

'And she said you slowly were able to put your father's death behind you.'

'With Robert's help.'

'Robert, with the beautiful wife and the incredible daughters. The earl, the beloved landlord.'

Simon nodded. His brother had been the perfect earl, the right mix of family man and imposing figure of authority.

'Then he died, and you were thrust back into mourning again, but this time there was no beloved brother to pull you out of it, and what was more you were expected to step into his shoes, to take his place.'

'I could never take his place.'

'But you were forced to. You became the earl, you took his seat in Parliament, you inherited all his properties, you were made to live the life which, only a few months before, your brother had.' Alice's voice softened, and she reached out and took his hand. 'Your mother thinks it was too much for you to bear, the idea that you were taking the life that should have been Robert's.'

'It was his life.'

'And she believes somewhere deep down you don't think you deserve to be alive when two great men, your father and your brother, were snatched away from this earth so early.'

Simon didn't say anything. It felt as though his heart were being squeezed inside his chest, and with every passing second the pain became more intense.

'It is why you will not even countenance a traditional marriage with me,' Alice said, her voice so low it was barely more than a whisper. 'You think that is a step too far. You have no choice but to be the earl and to take your seat in Parliament and to be the landlord to your tenants, but you can choose not to allow yourself any happiness, not to take that final part of Robert's life, the role of husband and father.'

'You have clearly thought about this a lot,' he murmured.

'I have thought of little else this past year. Your family have been struck by such tragedy, it is impossible to fathom the sorrow you must feel, yet I pity you not just for the loss of your father and brother but for your resolution that you do not deserve the happiness that they once had just because only you now survive.'

'I do not want your pity.'

Her fingers danced over the back of his hand, and he glanced up involuntarily. Alice looked agitated, as if she were about to burst into tears, but he did not have the emotional reserve to even think about comforting her right now.

With an air of desolate determination, she blinked back the tears. 'You do not want anything from anyone, Simon. You want to walk through this world without your troubles touching anyone else, but we do not live in isolation. Every time you push people away, every time you run away from your problems, you are hurting someone else besides yourself. I don't want you to suffer, Simon, but I also want you to see that when you suffer so do the rest of us, each and every person who cares about you.'

Ever since his father's death, he had not wanted to be a burden. He had seen how the bereavement had devastated his mother, how much more responsibility his brother had had to shoulder. He had wanted to make their lives easier, and here was Alice showing him he had done the complete opposite. He knew she was right, that whilst he had tried to push away his own pain, he had inadvertently made things harder for the very people he was trying to protect.

Quickly he thumped on the roof of the carriage again, waiting for it to slow before he threw open the door and jumped out. It had not completely stopped, and he startled a couple who were strolling arm-in-arm down the street, but he found he could not bring himself to care. He slammed the carriage door shut and without another word strode off, desperate to put as much distance between himself and Alice as possible.

His head was spinning, and he drew in deep ragged breaths, wondering how she had so thoroughly summed up everything he felt about his brother's death and the life he now lived.

Chapter Fifteen

Alice hated the silence in the house as she paced the floor of the drawing room. She had not meant to upset Simon, but once she had started trying to make him see what he was doing to himself she had been unable to stop.

Now it was eight hours later and Simon was still not home.

'You've probably made him run all the way back to Italy,' she muttered to herself.

Alice wished she had held her tongue. Simon was still grief-stricken from the death of his father and brother and reeling from the uncertainty of whether he suffered from the same condition that might strike him down at any moment. What she had said in the carriage was like sticking a knife in an already-wounded man. She was not proud of her actions, even though her words had been true.

She groaned. It had come from a selfish place, a need to lash out, as she had realised that Simon was never going to see her as anything more than a burden. Perhaps one he could develop a friendship with, but a burden all the same. When he had been quietly supportive in the orphanage, she had understood how much she yearned for a deeper relationship with this man. As much as she could tell herself she wished to safeguard her independence and protect herself from him hurting her by disappearing again, deep down she knew she wanted more.

'You are a fool,' she chided herself. Her outburst had only served to push him away and hurt him.

There was a noise from outside, and Alice stopped her pacing immediately. She had sent the servants to bed long ago, resolving to wait up herself to see if Simon returned. It was past two o'clock in the morning, and she had almost given up hope.

Alice rushed to the front door and opened it, jumping back as Simon half stumbled, half fell inside. He twisted as he fell and landed on his bottom, looking up at her and giving her a lopsided smile.

For a moment Alice didn't move, too stunned to do anything more than stare.

'Good evening, my beautiful wife,' Simon said, slurring his words.

'You're drunk.'

'I may have had one or two little glasses of whisky.' He tried to stand, but his feet got tangled, and he ended up where he had started on the floor.

'I have been so worried about you.' She took a deep breath, knowing she would have to apologise again in the morning when he was sober, but needing to get the words out now as well. 'I'm so sorry for what I said, Simon. It was unforgiveable.'

He tried to stand again, and this time managed to get to his feet, stumbling slightly as he moved. Alice reached out and steadied him, and he wrapped an arm around her shoulder.

'You smell nice,' he said, burying his face in her hair and inhaling deeply. 'You always smell nice.'

'I think we had better get you to bed,' she said as he reached up and plucked a pin out of her hair.

'You have such beautiful hair.' With clumsy fingers he pulled out a couple more pins, allowing the soft waves to cascade over her shoulders. 'You should wear it loose all the time. You look like a goddess.'

'You are very effusive when you are drunk.'

He grinned at her. 'Truthful. I'm truthful when I'm drunk.'

'Do you think you can manage the stairs?'

'Of course,' he said, almost tripping over his own feet and looking up at her guiltily. 'Perhaps with your help.'

Slowly they climbed the stairs, pausing halfway up for Simon to rest his head on her shoulder and declare she had the prettiest shoulders in the world.

Once upstairs they started along the hallway, passing the door to the master bedroom that was still Alice's. Simon reached out for the door-handle and opened it, pulling her in that direction.

'You don't sleep here,' she said, trying to pull him back into the hall, but her small stature put her at a disadvantage.

'We should sleep together,' he murmured. 'We are married. There is nothing wrong with it.'

'Do not jest, Simon.'

'I am completely serious,' he slurred, looking at her intently. 'What man wouldn't want to fall asleep with you in his arms?'

He had pulled her farther into the room now, and Alice looked back dubiously at the door.

'You can sleep here tonight. I will take your bedroom.'

'Stay with me, Miss James.'

'Alice,' she corrected him.

She stumbled back and sat down on the edge of the bed, almost sliding off onto the floor. Twice he reached down to try to pull his boots off, and twice he missed.

'Let me,' she said, placing a hand on his chest to stop him from bending down again. He caught hold of her wrist, his fingers caressing the delicate skin. For a moment she did not move, allowing herself to enjoy the caress. These last few days she had found thoughts of her husband touching her had crept into her mind unbidden far more than she would like to admit. It was typical that it took far too many glasses of whisky for her fantasy to become reality.

Brusquely she shrugged him off and bent down to pull off his boots.

'Thank you,' he murmured, lying back on the bed.

'No, no, no,' Alice said quickly, knowing if he fell asleep like this he would be uncomfortable and his clothes almost certainly ruined. 'We need to get you out of your jacket and cravat at the very least.'

'You want to see me naked, Alice,' he murmured, a smile on his face but his eyes closed.

She remained silent, putting her energy into helping him sit back up and then manoeuvring the jacket from his shoulders. His movements were uncoordinated, and it took far longer than it should, but eventually he was just in his shirt and trousers.

'Let's get you into bed,' she said, figuring he could sleep comfortably enough in the remaining clothes.

'I'm not undressed,' he murmured, and as she watched, he pulled his shirt over his head revealing the toned torso underneath. Although she had only ever seen him clothed, Alice knew he had a lean, muscled physique. Even through the layers of his shirt and jacket, the few times they had danced she had been able to feel the power he held in his body. Now, though, with his upper body bared in moonlight, she paused, her eyes raking over his half-naked form.

Alice felt something stir inside her, and she had to resist the urge to reach out and trail her fingers across his skin. In the state he was in, he would invite her in, forgetting about all the reasons he did not want to be intimate with her, but she would not do that to him, no matter how much she craved his touch.

'Let's get you into bed,' she said again, adopting her best schoolmistress voice and trying to pretend she was completely unaffected by him.

Somehow she managed to get him standing so she could pull back the sheets and then help him climb into bed. As she leaned over to ensure the pillows were comfortable under his head, his arm reach out and caught her around the waist.

'Don't leave me, Alice,' he said, his touch gentle but firm.

'I'll just be along the hall.'

'Stay with me tonight. You are my wife.'

'In name only,' she said, regretting the sharpness of her words immediately, but thankfully Simon did not seem to notice.

'There's space for you right here,' he said, and with a firm pull he tumbled her into bed beside him.

Alice let out a low cry of surprise and was about to sit up when Simon rolled over and flung his arm across her, pinning her in place. His face nuzzled into her neck, his lips brushing against her skin.

'Have I told you that you smell delicious?' he mumbled.

'You did mention it on the stairs.'

He murmured something incomprehensible, and then with his lips against her skin and his arm thrown possessively over her body, his breathing deepened.

'Simon,' Alice whispered, wriggling from side to side, unable to believe he had fallen asleep so quickly.

There was no response. She stilled, considering her predicament. The right thing to do would be to slip out from under his arm and leave him to sleep alone. She could spend the night in his bed; his room was comfortable and his bed made up and inviting. Yet something made her want to stay. Alice knew Simon was only being affectionate because he was in his cups. Tomorrow in the cold light of day, he would probably regret his actions, but tonight he had wanted her. This past year she had craved affection, craved the touch of another person, especially whilst she was in London. At least in Northumberland she received the occasional embrace from her sister-in-law or nieces, but here she was the lady of the house and so far above everyone else in social status there was no contact whatsoever.

Alice closed her eyes for a moment and wondered if she were being completely foolish, but it was merely a cuddle, one warm body pressed against another, nothing more. Tomorrow she could tell Simon she had been trapped by his arm over her waist, and it wouldn't be entirely untrue.

Deciding she would allow herself to have this one chaste night with her husband in their marital bed, Alice closed her eyes and tried to quieten her racing thoughts.

In all his thirty-three years, Simon had only been blindingly drunk a handful of times, normally after celebrations where drink after drink had been on offer and his spirits high. He thought back to the night after his graduation, surrounded by friends, toasting the end of their time at university. The memory gave him a momentary warm feeling, and he luxuriated in it for a few seconds before returning to the matter in hand.

'You're not a young pup anymore,' he muttered to himself. Ten years ago he could have drunk twice as much and not felt the room tilt around him the next day, but now his body was protesting, and he would probably pay for his excesses the entire day, or at the very least until he could get a strong cup of coffee inside him.

As he lay in bed, eyes firmly closed to guard against the room spinning, he realised he was not alone. There was a warm body in the bed next to him, soft and smooth, and he was pressed at least partially against her.

His eyes shot open, and he took in the red hair spread across the pillow and the peaceful face of his wife as she slept. She looked contented, happy even, and as he watched, she burrowed farther down into the pillow, her body shifting and pressing against him.

For a moment Simon was too shocked to move. She was in a sensible cotton nightgown with a dressing gown overtop, but at some point in the night the material had ridden up to reveal her legs and, above them, the hint of her buttocks. Up higher his hand rested across her waist, fingers splayed, the tips brushing against her breast.

Simon felt a surge of desire almost overwhelm him. He had always found his wife attractive, but lying in bed next to her, her warm body pressed against his, was unbearable. He wanted to lower his lips to hers and kiss her until she woke, and then strip the sensible nightdress from her body and enjoy every inch of her.

A sensible man would move away, but Simon could not bring himself to roll over. With a great effort he thought back to the night before. Alice did not look like she had been ravaged, her nightclothes were not torn or discarded, and she slept peacefully beside him.

Slowly the events of the previous evening came back to him. He retraced his steps from his gentlemen's club where he had spent half the afternoon trying to drown out the echo of Alice's words with a bottle of whisky. Later he had moved on to less salubrious establishments and had continued drinking where no one knew him.

He remembered stumbling home and Alice waiting for him, the rest of the house in darkness, and finally he remembered her helping him upstairs to bed.

Gently he pressed a kiss against the back of her head. She couldn't know how much he desired her, how every day he dreamed about scooping her into his arms and making her into his true wife. It was torture being so close and being unable to act on the desire that surged through him.

She was right in her assessment of him the day before, although her delivery of the stinging truths had left a lot to be desired. He wouldn't allow them to become close for two reasons. The first was as he had told her when he'd returned: he did not know when he might suddenly die, killed by the same affliction that had suddenly taken his father and his brother. He did not want to build a relationship with Alice only to pull it all away from her when his inevitable death came.

The second reason was something he thought had remained hidden deep inside, this feeling that he had stepped into Robert's life. He had the title, the seat in Parliament, the estate and all the properties, the responsibility of being the earl. All the things Robert had relished and enjoyed. It would be too much if Simon had a happy marriage and children too, those things that his brother had cherished the most.

'Not so hidden,' he murmured quietly. It would seem his mother had guessed what stopped him from settling down as an earl was expected to, what drove him away from a conventional marriage to live a life of loneliness.

He wished it wasn't the case, and he knew Robert would never begrudge him happiness, but he couldn't help feeling as though he had stolen his brother's life.

Next to him Alice shifted and pressed herself even closer against him, giving a little sigh of contentment. He knew she wanted more from their marriage, that despite having built a life for herself here with her charities and position in society, she craved human touch and affection. He had seen the way she glanced at him, the desire in her eyes, and part of him responded in the same way.

With his free hand he reached out and gently stroked her hair, allowing himself to imagine for a moment a life where he gave in to his desire. Long mornings spent in bed together, snatched kisses in public, walking hand in hand through Hyde Park. Skipping dinner in favour of returning to the bedroom and trying to quench the insatiable desire they felt.

It was a tempting picture, and with her warm body pressed against him he almost gave in, but nothing had changed, not really. Alice might know of the pain and turmoil that raged inside him, but that did not lessen it.

She let out a soft sigh and then wriggled a little, and as he watched, her eyelids flickered open. She gave him a sleepy smile, not really registering she was pressed against her husband in bed, but after a few seconds her eyes widened, and she scrabbled to sit up, pulling the bedcovers around her.

He hair was loosed down her back, and he vaguely remembered leaning in and plucking some of the pins out the night before, yet he certainly wouldn't have had the dexterity to remove them all. That meant she had taken some out herself. Equally, even if he had been the one to pull her into bed, she would not have remained trapped indefinitely. At some point she had decided to stay, decided to spend the night with her husband, removed the rest of the pins from her hair and fallen asleep in his arms.

'Good morning,' he said, speaking softly, aware that soon his head would begin pounding from the aftereffects of the alcohol.

'Good morning,' Alice said eventually.

'Thank you for helping me to bed last night.'

She inclined her head, unable to meet his eye for a second. 'How do you feel?'

'Like I drank far too much whisky yesterday,' he said with a half-smile. 'Unsurprisingly.'

She looked at him, biting her lip and screwing up the bed-sheets in her hands.

'I'm so sorry,' she blurted out, a look of anguish on her face. 'What I said to you yesterday was unforgiveable. I should have kept my thoughts to myself. It is none of my business why you do not wish to have a conventional wife or a family. It should be enough that you tell me that you don't.'

'Nonsense,' he said softly. 'The way we entered into this marriage might have been unorthodox, but I cannot continue pretending I do not have a wife.' He reached out and placed his hand next to hers so their fingers were touching. 'If anyone has the right to talk to me of these things it is you.'

'I went about it the wrong way.'

'That I will not deny,' he said, softening the reproof with a smile, 'but I do not believe your intention was malicious. Indeed, I think it came from a place of affection, which is remarkable, given how I have held you at arm's-length since I returned.' He looked down now to where their arms touched and wished he could reach out and take her hand in his own, but despite the desire he felt, despite the affection and respect, he still could not rid himself of the belief that he did not deserve the happiness that such a union would bring.

Alice looked at him sadly. 'You do deserve happiness, Simon. I know it doesn't mean much coming from me, a near stranger, but I have listened to what your family have said about you this past year. I have heard of your devotion to your nieces and how you coaxed Sylvia from a very dark place after her father died. I have heard how you supported Maria and ensured she didn't have to think of the practicalities when she was left widowed with three young children.' She paused, looking at him almost pleadingly before pressing on. 'Then, there are your actions when it comes to me. We were both foolish at the Midsummer's Eve ball, but you would not have suffered the consequences, especially with your plans already made to leave England. Yet despite having an easy way out, you did not hesitate to upend your decision to ensure I was protected. You gave me your name and a life of comfort and opportunity. Do you know how few men would do that for a woman they barely knew?' She shook her head, not waiting for an answer. 'You swooped in and rescued me, Simon, from a life of shame and scandal, when my best hope was that a man I hated would consent to marry me. How could I not fall a little in love with you?'

This made him look up sharply, and Alice held up a placating hand.

'Do not fear, I do not deny over the past year I have dreamed of you returning from Italy, telling me you could not bear to be away from me, but since your return you have made it clear there will be no intimacy between us. We shall live our lives like two spinster siblings, chaste with a moderate affection. I have heard what you have told me over and over again.'

'I have been a little blunt, haven't I?'

She smiled at that. 'Perhaps I have needed the bluntness.'

'I cannot change how I feel about Robert,' Simon said.

'I know.' Her expression was sad but not surprised. He

felt a sudden surge of anger, directed towards himself. Here he was in bed beside a beautiful woman, a woman he had could not stop thinking about kissing, and all he had done these past few days was make her miserable.

'If you think you could allow yourself to be happy with someone else, I would understand,' Alice said softly. 'I know I was not the woman you would have chosen for a wife, and if you wish to take a mistress I will not object.'

'You doubt my attraction to you,' he said, his voice low.

She looked at him in surprise, and Simon felt something shift inside him. If he were to reach out and pull her to him, there would be nothing illicit about it. They were husband and wife, and Alice could not hide the fact that she was attracted to him. The only person standing in the way of the desire they both felt was him.

He felt the familiar guilt he was hit with every time he contemplated something enjoyable, but this time he pushed it down. He wasn't proposing he live a normal, full life with Alice, not like Robert had experienced with his wife, just that he and Alice enjoy the occasional bit of affection.

'Do not doubt my attraction to you.'

He looped a firm arm around her waist, feeling the warmth of her skin through the layers of her nightclothes. Alice's body was stiff for a second, and then she let out a little moan and relaxed against him.

Before he could talk himself out of it, Simon kissed her, a kiss filled with all the pent-up desire and passion that had been surging through him since his return. He gripped Alice gently, and manoeuvred her into his lap, loving the way she felt as she wrapped her legs around him.

Her lips were soft and sweet, and he kissed her deeply, as if searching for something he had lost long ago.

'You do not know how many times I have dreamed of doing this,' he said, pulling away for a second to kiss the soft skin of her neck. She shivered at the touch of his lips on her skin and pulled him closer.

He wanted to take his time and enjoy her, to show her pleasure in so many different ways, yet he also felt a frantic need to do this quickly in case the rational part of his mind took over at any point.

'Simon,' she whispered, invoking his name like he was a demigod. He kissed her again, long and deep, his hands caressing her back.

'This needs to come off,' he said, gripping the thin material of her nightgown. Without protest Alice slipped an arm from her dressing gown and then wriggled out of it completely. Now there was only her nightgown separating their bodies. She shifted on his lap, brushing against his hardness as she lifted herself up and he caught hold of the hem of the garment. Before either of them could come to their senses, he lifted the nightdress over her head and threw it on the floor beside the bed.

For a moment they both stilled, Alice with a look of apprehension in her eyes that reminded him that she might be a married woman in the eyes of society, but that she was still very much an innocent.

Slowly he lifted a hand and trailed a finger from the notch between her collarbones down between her breasts.

'You are beautiful, Alice,' he said.

Her instinct was to cover herself with her arms, wrapping them round her body, and he cursed himself for his part in making her feel unattractive or unwanted. Nothing could be further from the truth. Right now he could not understand how he had allowed himself to be apart from her for so long.

Gently he pressed her arms back to her sides and trailed his fingers over her chest again, loving the way her breath caught in her throat as his hand brushed against her breast.

'You're teasing me,' she said, a note of accusation in her voice.

'I am building the anticipation,' he said, smiling.

'Another way of saying *teasing*.'

'Would you prefer it if I just dove straight in?' he said, leaning forward and taking her nipple into his mouth, making her gasp with pleasure and shock.

Alice let out an incomprehensible moan, and he felt her body stiffen underneath him before slowly she relaxed, letting her head drop to his shoulder.

He pulled away, kissing her again and resuming his slow, gentle caress of her body.

'You have the softest skin I have ever felt,' he murmured, circling from the top of her chest around her breasts and back again. He repeated the movement again and again until he could feel the anticipation. Carefully he flipped her over so she was lying on her back on the bed, and he held himself above her, lowering his lips to meet her body. He took his time, trailing kisses across her breasts and over her abdomen as she writhed underneath him, the heat building between them.

He stroked her thighs as he kissed her, slowly coaxing her to relax.

'What are you doing to me?' Alice whispered as he

moved even lower, feeling her tense and push forwards involuntarily as he kissed her thighs.

He didn't answer her; instead, he trailed kisses up her thighs and then without any further warning kissed her in her most private place. Alice let out a shocked yelp, her hands scrabbling at his head.

'What are you doing, Simon?'

'I would have thought that obvious.'

'I did not know...'

'That you could be kissed there? No, I suppose you would not. Can I show you how good it can feel?'

With only a moment's hesitation she nodded, and Simon lowered his head, loving the way her hips came up to meet him. She was responsive to his every touch, and it wasn't long before he saw she was gripping the bed-sheets either side of her with her hands as if clinging on for her life.

Alice's breathing quickened and then she clamped her legs together, letting out a deep moan.

Simon raised himself up and pushed his trousers down, holding himself above Alice before he pressed against her. Slowly he entered her, feeling her body rise to meet his, and then he was fully buried inside her.

He held in place for a moment, his eyes meeting Alice's, and then he withdrew, knowing he had to go slow for her, but it took every ounce of his self-control. Gradually he increased the speed of his thrusts, lowering his lips to brush against hers and loving the way her fingers raked down his back. Beneath him he felt her tense and tighten and then let out a moan of pleasure as she climaxed, the look of ecstasy on her face and the tightness that engulfed him enough to push him over the edge.

Quickly he withdrew and finished on the sheets, even in the moment of passion in control enough to know he could not risk her getting pregnant.

He moved off Alice, coming in behind her and pulling her into an embrace. He couldn't see her face, but her body did not feel fully relaxed, and he wondered if she was already regretting their moment of intimacy.

Eventually she turned to face him, her eyes searching his for something he worried she would not find. Without a word she turned back, tucking her body close to his, and pulling his arm around her. She laced her fingers through his, and he held her tight.

Chapter Sixteen

Alice had been surprised that she'd slept again, a deep slumber that had not been disturbed by Simon rising at some point, and she was disappointed to find herself alone when she woke. She wondered if their intimacy had been enough to drive him away completely, out of London, perhaps even out of the country, she and glanced over at the little writing desk in the corner to see if she could spot a hastily scrawled note.

There was no note, and a few minutes later the door to the bedroom opened and Simon walked in carrying a tray of coffee and a couple of newspapers under one arm.

'You're awake,' he said with a smile.

Alice would never admit how much it pleased her that he was still here.

'What time is it?'

'After ten. I checked with Miss Stick, and she tells me you have no engagements until your dinner party with the Hampshires this evening.'

Simon was fully dressed, and he showed no outward signs of his heavy night of drinking, although once he had poured the coffee he took a tentative sip before deciding to take a full cup.

'I brought you the papers,' he said. 'We are mentioned in the gossip rag.'

Alice's eyes widened. She had been featured many times before, but in recent months only small comments about what dress she had decided to wear or who she had danced with, nothing more interesting than that, but from Simon's tone she could tell today was different.

'Third paragraph down.'

She let her eyes drift over the first two paragraphs quickly, then read aloud.

'*Lord Westcroft made a return to London this week, much to the surprise of society and to his wife. Lady Westcroft was left looking shocked at the Livingstones' ball when her husband waltzed in and swept her onto the dance floor. One has to wonder if the errant Lord Westcroft thinks of his wife at all—at the very least he does not seem to include her in his travel plans.*'

She eyed Simon carefully. It was more a criticism of him than her, and not entirely untrue even if it was an unflattering view of the situation.

'They are not wrong. I did just waltz into the Livingstones' ball and surprise you. It must have been unsettling for you.'

Alice blinked, pulling the sheets up a little farther to cover her nakedness. *This* was what they were going to talk about now? After everything that had happened yesterday and this morning?

Pointedly she set the paper on the bed and looked at him expectantly. Simon sipped his coffee, pretending he didn't feel her eyes on him and then sighed.

'You wish to talk about this morning.'

'We *need* to talk about this morning.'

Simon cleared his throat and then for a long time did not say anything at all.

'Simon,' she prompted him eventually.

'I spent a long time thinking yesterday after our…discussion,' he said slowly. 'And I have to acknowledge that on many points you are correct. I do feel guilty about living the life my brother should have, and I shy away from following the same path as him in the parts that are not essential. I had vowed never to marry, but when we met we set into motion a chain of events that led us to the altar. It did not matter too much, for the marriage was not to be like Robert's, not a love match.'

Alice hugged her knees to her, wondering if she was strong enough to hear what he had to say.

'I am not trying to punish myself, or you, in any way, Alice. I know my father's and brother's deaths were not my fault, yet I cannot help the guilt I feel that I am still here whilst they are not.'

'I understand that can be quite common amongst people where one person survives a tragedy when others close to them have died.'

'It was hard hearing that everyone close to me had worked out what was going on in far better detail than I had,' he said quietly. 'I think that is why I was so upset yesterday. I thought what I was doing wasn't affecting other people too much, but I was wrong.'

Alice felt like they were reaching some ultimatum, some declaration of how he truly felt and what he wanted from his future.

'I cannot deny the desire I feel for you, Alice. I think that was obvious this morning.'

Alice felt her heart sink. As unlikely as it was, she

had hoped for a declaration of love, a suggestion that they make their marriage a conventional one where they enjoyed each other's company to the fullest. She chided herself for getting her hopes up once again. She was too naïve in the ways of the heart, and she needed to start protecting herself better.

'What do you propose we do?'

Simon sighed. 'I am not sure we can live in the same house and not end up in a similar situation as we did this morning.'

'You wish to leave?'

'No,' he said quickly. 'I do not. Yet I cannot offer you what a husband should in these circumstances.'

Love. He could not offer her love. Even if he stayed, he would be holding part of himself back, making sure he held her at arm's-length to deny himself the happiness they could have.

She pressed her lips together, wishing she could find the words to tell him how she felt, how it hurt to have him stand here and tell her that, despite the fact they were married and they both desired one another and cared for one another, he could not allow himself to build a mutually loving relationship with her. She should reject his unspoken proposal, but she thought of how her body craved his touch, of how happy she had felt in the moments of their lovemaking.

She had entered into this marriage after Simon had told her he would be dead within the year and she would be free to marry a man of her choosing, a man who could love her. That wasn't going to happen now, and if the doctors had got things wrong it might never be the case. She had forty years of marriage stretching out in front of her with a man who could not love her, and she could not seek that comfort elsewhere. At least if they had a physical relationship, she could slake some of her craving for intimacy with Simon's touch.

'We continue as before,' Alice said, decisively. 'Companionship, friendship, they are our focus, but with the added benefit of sharing a bed whenever we both choose.'

'You would be comfortable with that arrangement?'

'We are married. There is nothing wrong with it,' Alice said firmly. 'We are both adults with desires and needs, and I think it safe to say we both find the other attractive.'

'Indeed,' Simon murmured.

'Then, it is settled. I know not to expect a declaration of love from you, and you are happy to give me the freedom I have enjoyed for the last year to make my own decisions.'

'I feel as though we should shake hands,' Simon murmured.

'There is no need for that,' Alice said quickly. Despite the agreement she had just proposed, she felt as though she needed some privacy to pull apart what she had just agreed to. It was all very well telling Simon that she would not develop feelings for him, but if she were honest she was well past halfway to loving him already, flaws and all. 'Now, I need to wash and dress. Could you ring the bell for my lady's maid?'

Chapter Seventeen

It was growing dark when they stepped out of the carriage in front of Mr and Mrs Hampshire's house, Simon offering her his arm. Alice felt the spark that flowed between them as her body brushed against his and quickly tried to quell it. She'd spent the day trying to persuade herself she hadn't made the biggest mistake of her life, and now she was beginning to believe their decision might actually be for the best.

Simon had been attentive on the carriage ride to the Hampshires after a note had arrived that afternoon, inviting him to join the dinner party, and Alice was enjoying his company. For the past year she had always had to arrive alone at events like this, and it was pleasant to walk in on her husband's arm.

It was not to be a large affair, and in the drawing room Mrs Livingstone ensured they both had a drink before dinner. There were five other guests, all people Alice knew fairly well, including Lady Kennington and her husband, and a wealthy couple in their forties who had moved to London from Bath a year earlier with their eighteen-year-old daughter, Emma.

'Emma is going to play for us,' Mrs Hampshire announced, showing Alice and Simon to a small sofa to listen.

Emma Finn was a talented pianist, and she played a few pieces perfectly with no music in front of her. Alice found herself relaxing, sinking back into the cushions of the sofa and into her husband. Simon had an arm behind her, resting on the back of the sofa, but after a minute she felt his fingers gently caressing her neck. At first it was an occasional touch, a gentle stroke as she shifted in her seat, but as the other guests became focussed on Emma at the piano, his touch became bolder, and he began tracing circles on the soft skin of her neck, just below her ear.

Alice felt as though every inch of her skin was taut with anticipation, and as his touch intensified she could not follow the music. All she could think about was Simon's fingers dancing over her skin, imagining him dipping lower.

All too soon the music finished, and Alice had to shake herself from the daze she found herself in.

They were not seated next to each other at dinner, as was the custom, but Alice found it hard to concentrate on anything but the fleeting glances she shared with Simon across the table. He was directly opposite her, and she had to keep reminding herself it was not polite to just stare longingly at her husband all evening. She'd had her reservations about their new arrangement, but trying to bury her attraction for him would have been futile.

'What did you think of St Benedict's?' Lady Kennington asked her as the main courses were brought out. Alice started to answer and then felt Simon's foot tap her own under the table. She forced herself to concentrate.

'It is well-run. I liked Mrs Phillips, the matron. She seemed sensible and kind, and the children were polite and clean. But the orphanage was in a dire state, and I think they have very little funds available to them.'

'It is a good cause, is it not?'

'Very good. I have asked Mrs Phillips to put some thought into what she feels would be helpful from the London Ladies' Benevolent Society.' Alice was about to say more, but Simon was gently caressing her leg with his foot, and she was finding it difficult to concentrate.

'Are you feeling well, Lady Westcroft?' Lady Kennington enquired.

'A little warm, that is all,' Alice said quickly, resolutely not looking at her husband.

The rest of dinner followed in much the same way, with Alice trying to concentrate on the conversation around the table but being unable to think of anything but the man sitting across from her, imagining he was pushing her back onto the bed and making love to her. It felt like the meal went on for ages, and Alice was pleased when it was time to move back to the drawing room, with the men moving to another downstairs room for drinks and cards. After a minute of listening to Miss Finn on the piano, she quietly excused herself, muttering something about the ladies' retiring room. In truth she needed some time to herself.

There were candles lit in the hall, but it was dark compared to the drawing room, and as Alice made her way to the stairs she did not even think to look in the dark corners. She gasped as a figure stepped out from the shadows by the stairs, gripping her by the wrists and pressing her against the wall.

'Simon,' she whispered, her heart pounding.

'You mean to torture me,' he murmured in her ear.

'Torture you?'

'You look ravishing tonight, and all I can think about...' He kissed her neck, making Alice gasp. 'You bring me somewhere I cannot touch you. I cannot even sit next to you.'

His lips were hot on her skin, and she felt a shudder of pleasure run through her body. It didn't matter that they were standing in someone else's hall, it didn't matter that at any moment someone could come out of one of the rooms and see them: all she could think of was Simon and where he would kiss her next.

'All I could think about all dinner was stripping you naked and lying you down on the dinner table.'

Alice gasped, picturing the scene. 'Not with everyone watching.'

'They would scatter soon enough. Good Lord, how do you always smell so good?'

'Simon, not the hair,' she said as he reached for one of her pins. 'I have to go back in there.'

He ran a hand down her side, over her waist and around to her buttocks and then lowered his lips to the bare skin of her upper chest. For a moment she forgot where they were and let out a moan that seemed to echo around the grand entrance hall.

'We need to get home,' he said, lifting his lips for just a second. 'Or we will never be invited to a dinner party with the Hampshires again.'

Before she could answer, he kissed her deeply, one hand still pinning both of hers above her head. He was gentle, but there was no denying he was much stronger than her, and she loved the way he held her against the wall, the cool wallpaper against her back.

'I will make my excuses,' Alice said, allowing herself one last kiss before she pulled away.

She paused before reentering the drawing room, aware that her cheeks were flushed and her clothes probably a little dishevelled. Thankfully, Miss Finn was still playing another masterful piece on the piano, and Alice was able to sidle up to their hostess and speak to her discreetly.

'I am awfully sorry, Mrs Hampshire, but I feel a little unwell. I think it best I return home.'

Mrs Hampshire looked at Alice with concern. 'You do look pink, my dear. Yes, go home at once, and get that housekeeper of yours to make a tincture.'

'Thank you for a wonderful evening.'

'Do you wish for me to send someone to accompany you home?'

'No, I am sure Lord Westcroft will be happy to come with me.'

Mrs Livingstone smiled indulgently. 'Of course. I forget you are still like newly-weds. Come, let us go fetch your husband.'

It felt like an eternity before they had bid everyone goodnight and the carriage had been brought round to the front door, but after a final wave to their hosts, Alice and Simon were alone.

Before he stepped up into the carriage Simon had a quiet word with the driver and then they were underway, travelling at a good pace through the quiet streets.

'I have instructed Drummond to keep circling around London until I alert him we wish to go home,' Simon said.

Alice's eyes widened, but before she could say any-thing Simon gently pulled her onto his lap.

'Where were we?'

'I think you were kissing me here,' Alice said, indi-cating the spot on her neck just below her ear. When he kissed her there it sent little jolts of pleasure all the way through her body.

'And I think my hands were here,' Simon said, slip-ping his hands underneath her and giving her buttocks a squeeze as he gave her a mock lascivious raise of his eyebrows.

She leaned forward and kissed him, losing herself in desire. It felt as though she were falling head first into paradise, and she didn't want to ever stop.

They kissed for a long time, then Alice shifted, snak-ing her hands down in between them to push at the waist-band of his trousers. He gathered her skirts up, and soon there was nothing between them. Alice positioned herself carefully, feeling the wonderful fullness as he entered her, and then she was lost as their bodies came together again and again until she cried out, and wave after wave of pleasure flooded through her.

Simon lifted her off him quickly before he, too, let out a low groan of pleasure.

For a long while neither of them spoke.

'You make me reckless,' she said eventually.

'I think it is the other way round,' Simon murmured. 'Take the Midsummer's Eve ball. I have spent the last ten years carefully avoiding any scandal that might tie me to a respectable young woman. A few hours in your company and I'm suggesting midnight dashes through the gardens and kissing you far too close to the house.'

Alice closed her eyes and remembered that night. It was the night that had changed the course of her life. When things got difficult, all she had to do was remind herself that she could have been unlucky enough to be married to vile Cousin Cecil. This arrangement with her husband was unusual and certainly not what she would have chosen for herself when she was a young girl dreaming of her perfect man, but it was better than a lifetime of repression as Cecil's wife.

'You look serious,' Simon said, leaning forward and stroking her forehead between her eyebrows. 'What are you thinking about?'

'How the course of my life changed completely in the space of one evening.'

'It did, didn't it?'

'I suppose none of us can know what life has in store for us.'

They lapsed into silence, and Alice wondered if Simon was thinking about all the uncertainty in his life. She wanted him to see that he was not the only one who did not know what would happen. He might have the same condition that had killed his father and his brother, but equally he might not. Even if he did, it might not strike him down for decades. There were so many dangers in life; people were caught up in unpredictable scenarios all the time. Simon had reason to be more worried than most, but it did not mean she agreed with his approach to hold everyone he loved at a distance in hope that they would not suffer as much when he did die.

She looked at him and bit her lip. Despite her stern words to herself and her best efforts, she knew she was falling in love with Simon. She felt more than desire, more than physical attraction. She wanted more than he could offer her. It was a sure way to get hurt, but it wasn't something under her conscious control.

Chapter Eighteen

The next week passed in a blur with one day running into the next. They spent a large proportion of their time in the bedroom. Simon could not keep his hands off Alice, wherever they were. He sought her out in the drawing room or at the breakfast table, and she was always as happy to kiss him as he was her. As the week progressed they stopped pretending to even try to do anything else and gave in to the pleasure of acting like newly-weds.

'I need to get dressed today,' Alice said on the morning of their eighth day together. 'Mrs Phillips from St Benedict's Orphanage sent a note yesterday saying she had spent some time thinking about what would be really helpful to the orphanage. She invited me to meet with her for an hour or so this afternoon.'

Simon frowned. 'I have an appointment with my solicitor that I cannot miss this afternoon, to go over a few land issues that have come up during my absence.'

Alice trailed her fingers over Simon's naked shoulder and then lowered her lips to kiss it absently. 'It does not matter. If Drummond takes me in the carriage I will be perfectly safe. I will ensure he drops me off right outside.'

'One of those street children had a knife.'

'I think that is probably true of many people in our beautiful city.'

'None of them have threatened you.'

'That is true.' She considered for a moment. 'How about I take Frank Smith with me? He is young and strong, and his background means he is used to the tricks and schemes of the street urchins.'

'I would prefer to come with you myself, but I suppose that is a fair compromise. With Drummond and Smith, you can hardly get into too much trouble.'

'I promise to go straight there and straight back,' Alice said, smiling. 'No matter how many pallid pickpockets I run into and feel sorry for.'

'No pallid pickpockets, and no diversions.'

She leaned in and kissed him, feeling a thrill of anticipation for the day ahead.

'I shall be back home around five, then we have dinner with the Dunns later.'

'Then, I have plenty of time to persuade you we should send our apologies and have dinner at home.'

'You would choose to stay home every night of the week,' Alice said as Simon's arm snaked around her waist.

'Tell me you'd rather spend the evening with dull old Mr Dunn droning on about the time he almost joined the navy or Mrs Dunn trying to pretend she has early knowledge of the fashions coming out of Paris, and I will admit defeat now.'

'You are being uncharitable,' she said as he pulled her down for a kiss.

'You have a choice. Either we can spend the evening

with the Dunns or we can cancel and I will count how many times I can kiss your body before you beg me for something more.'

'You are not playing fair, Simon,' Alice said, mock reproval in her voice. 'You get to persuade me with kisses. Mr Dunn only gets his tales about the navy.'

He kissed her again.

'When the stakes are this high, it is best not to play fair.'

Reluctantly Alice stood and moved over to the mirror. She needed to go to the modiste today too, after postponing her appointment for a fitting of a new dress earlier in the week.

'I will consider your proposition, but now I am going to have to insist you leave. I have neglected my errands for too long.'

Simon stood, picking up his crumpled shirt from the chair where she had thrown it the previous evening, and pulling it over his head.

'You wound me with the ease with which I am cast out, discarded,' Simon said, his hand on the door-handle. 'Until tonight, my sweet.'

The rest of Alice's day was productive, but she had the feeling of wanting to rush through everything so she could return home to Simon. It was a ridiculous idea, for he wouldn't be home from the solicitor until after she had finished at the orphanage.

At three o'clock she instructed Drummond to take her to St Benedict's. Frank Smith sat on the narrow bench at the front of the carriage beside Drummond, primed to step in if there were any trouble.

The journey through London was uneventful, and

before long the carriage stopped outside the orphanage. It was an overcast day, and the slums looked even less inviting with their narrow streets in shadow.

'I shall be about an hour. Keep vigilant,' Alice instructed Drummond and Smith before knocking on the door of the orphanage.

Mrs Phillips welcomed her in and showed her through to the small room at the back of the building that acted as the matron's bedroom and office. It was sparsely furnished, with bare floorboards and nothing on the walls. There was a single bed in the corner of the room and two straight-back chairs by a little table. At the foot of the bed was a small trunk, and on the back of the door a hook for a coat. Mrs Phillips might be matron of the establishment, but her accommodation wasn't much more comfortable than that of the children in her care.

Alice knew the woman's role carried huge responsibility but did not attract a large salary, especially in a small, poor establishment like St Benedict's. Mrs Phillips would eat the same food as the children and might even be restricted in when and why she could leave the premises.

One of the girls brought in a heavy teapot on a tray with two cups, and Mrs Phillips served Alice.

'Thank you for coming, Lady Westcroft. I have been thinking about what you suggested,' Mrs Phillips said as she handed a cup to Alice.

They talked for more than an hour, discussing all the issues Mrs Phillips had noted down, from small things like the purchase of more slate boards for the classroom to much larger concerns such as sanitation and access to clean water. By the end of their discussion, Alice felt exhausted but excited to share Mrs Phillips's ideas with the London Ladies' Benevolent Society.

At five o'clock, she bid Mrs Phillips farewell and stepped out into the warm late-afternoon air. Alice was preoccupied, wondering how best to present all the issues to the other ladies and she stepped out into the street without looking.

It was uncommon to see people on horseback in this part of the city. Most people travelled on foot, and those who had to pass through preferred the safety of a carriage. She looked up too late: the horse was almost upon her, and Alice saw the rider pull on the reins sharply, causing the horse to rear up in fright. Hooves thundered past her face, missing by mere inches as a firm hand on her shoulder pulled her backwards to safety.

The whole incident lasted less than a few seconds, but Alice felt as though she had been running for a whole hour. Her heart squeezed in her chest, and her breathing was ragged and uneven. The man on horseback called something incomprehensible and probably unkind and carried on along the street as if nothing had happened.

As she regained her composure Alice turned to the person who had pulled her back.

'Thank you—' she began, the words dying in her throat. Standing very close, a malicious glint in his eye, was the man who had watched them the time she and Simon had come to the orphanage.

'You're welcome, miss. Can't have a pretty lady like yourself trampled under a horse's hooves, brains splattered about the cobbles,' he said, his voice low so only she could hear.

Alice swallowed and glanced down, feeling a cold

chill spread through her as she caught the glint of metal in his hand. He was holding a small knife in the narrow space between their bodies, the tip pointed at her abdomen. The metal was dull and looked well-used, and Alice thought she saw a crust of blood around the hilt.

'Don't call out,' the man said calmly. 'Your best chance is if those two fools on top of the carriage do not come over to see what is happening.'

Glancing up, she saw Drummond's face. As yet he was not climbing down from the carriage, but he was looking over at her with an expression of puzzled concern on his face. Alice knew it would only be a matter of seconds until he was climbing down to investigate why she hadn't crossed the road and got into the safety of the carriage.

'Now, I did not have to save your life there, miss, but I am an upstanding citizen, and I think a good deed like that deserves a reward.'

Alice nodded, wishing she had brought her coin purse so she could have just handed it over without any delay.

'I do not carry money on my person,' she said truthfully. It was foolish to carry money in areas such as this where half the population were desperate enough to steal if the temptation were right.

'That is a shame, miss. I suppose we'll have to think of something else.' He looked her over, grunting as he saw she was not wearing a necklace or earrings. The only jewellery she had was the wedding band on her finger. 'You'd better start with that gold ring,' he said, motioning at it with his knife.

Alice looked down, reluctant to part with the ring Simon had given her on the day of their wedding. It was symbolic of so much, and she did not want to part with it, but she knew compliance was the best way to walk away unscathed from this situation.

She reached down with her right hand to try to pull the ring off, grimacing at the resistance. As she worked on pulling it over the knuckle, she saw Drummond and Smith finally realise there was something wrong. They moved fast for men trained as household servants, dashing across the road to come to her aid. The man who was stealing from her glanced up and saw them coming, reaching out to grab the ring from Alice. As he did so, Smith arrived and went to throw his whole body weight at the thief. The culprit ducked under Smith's arm and quickly struck out, clearing a path through the middle of them. To Alice's dismay he disappeared into the crowd within seconds.

'Thank you,' she said, turning to Drummond and Smith. They were both looking at her in horror. Slowly, not wanting to know what sight awaited her, she looked down. A bloom of blood was spreading across her pale blue dress, staining the material and seeping out around the blade of the knife that was still buried in her abdomen. 'There's a knife,' she said, feeling her whole body stagger to the left at the sight of the blood and the thought of the wound that must be underneath.

Instinctively her hand gripped the handle of the knife, thinking to pull it out, but Drummond reached out to stop her.

'Leave it,' he said forcefully. 'We need to get you back home and then a doctor can remove the knife. Do not even think about touching it.' Her abdomen was starting to throb and hurt, and she marvelled that she had not felt the knife slide into her flesh.

Drummond lowered his shoulder and half carried, half dragged Alice to the carriage. Carefully he helped her inside, instructing her to lie across the seats and avoid any unnecessary movement.

The journey back home seemed to take for ever, with Alice feeling every jolt of the carriage and every corner they rounded. Drummond was driving fast, aware Alice was inside the carriage bleeding, and no doubt eager to get her home before she lost so much blood she breathed her last breath. Frank sat opposite her, looking young and scared, his arm placed strategically to ensure she did not tumble from her seat.

As the carriage slowed, Alice saw Drummond jump down calling out as he did so, and the next thing she saw was Simon's anxious face.

'Alice, what happened?'

She tried to lift her head, but the world tilted and shifted under her, so instead she closed her eyes and let someone else tell him.

Outside she could hear Simon ordering someone to run for the doctor and also the barber-surgeon. Alice tried to protest: she had heard terrible stories about these barber-surgeons and the things they did in terms of professional interest. She did not want to endure an agonising procedure, her only comfort a little strong alcohol beforehand.

Tears began running down her cheeks as Simon carefully looked back into the carriage.

'Stay here with me, my love,' he said softly, reaching

out and taking her hand. Now half the front of her dress was bloodstained, and it hurt every time she moved.

Simon carefully climbed into the carriage and slipped his arms underneath her, lifting her ever so gently. He moved slowly, his eyes fixed on her face so he could see if there was any increase in pain as he carried her. The hardest part was getting out of the carriage, but once he extricated them, Simon could move more quickly. He carried her into the house and straight up the stairs to the bedroom they had shared this past week.

Miss Stick helped to position her in bed, pulling back the bed-sheets and then tucking them around Alice's legs, and then she hurried out to organise anything the doctor might need.

Simon stayed with her, kneeling by the side of the bed as if he were a child saying his prayers, his hand holding hers tight.

Alice closed her eyes, feeling suddenly weary despite the pain.

'Stay awake, my sweet,' Simon said softly but firmly. 'It is important you stay awake.'

With great effort she forced her eyes open. They felt like they had heavy weights attached to her eyelids, and all she wanted to do was surrender to the pull of sleep.

A few minutes later she heard the doctor arrive, and Simon quickly explained the situation. She had not met the man before, having been in good health since arriving in London, and was pleased to see a reassuring, sensible face looking down at her.

'We need to remove Lady Westcroft's clothing so I can see the wound fully before I attempt to take out the knife,' Dr Black said, motioning for Miss Stick to come forward from her position by the door. 'We need scissors, as sharp as possible, to cut away the material. I dare not try to lift her garments over her head.'

Miss Stick returned a few moments later with sharp scissors and leaned over Alice. Her normally composed demeanour had cracked, and Alice could see tears in the housekeeper's eyes.

'Let me, Miss Stick,' Simon said quietly, taking the scissors from the woman.

He worked slowly but steadily, instructing Miss Stick to hold the material of her dress taut as he cut it. The bodice part of her dress was thicker and Alice felt the scissors jolt and stop a few times, but after a minute the fabric was laid open to reveal her chemise and petti-coats underneath.

Despite her predicament, Alice felt a little self-conscious. No doubt in the course of his job Dr Black was accustomed to seeing the naked form, but the only man who had ever seen her naked was her husband, and she suddenly had the urge to cover herself with her hands.

'Be still, Alice,' Simon murmured reassuringly as he gripped the hem of her chemise and began sliding the scissors along the material. 'There is only you and I and Miss Stick here with the doctor.'

Once Alice's chemise was cut, Miss Stick hurried forward and arranged a sheet over her chest to help pre-serve Alice's dignity, and then the doctor stepped for-ward to look at the wound.

The dagger was still embedded in her abdomen at the level of her navel, but far to the right in the space be-tween the bottom of her ribs and the bones that marked the top of her pelvis. With every movement the wound stung and sent a jolt of pain through her body. The doctor took his time inspecting the wound and then moved away from the bed to talk to Simon.

'I wish to hear,' Alice called, surprised at how weak her voice sounded. The doctor looked over, a serious expression on his face, but Simon placed a hand on the man's elbow and guided him closer to the bed.

'It will be dangerous to remove the knife, but we must for the wound to begin to heal,' Dr Black said, his expression grave. 'I believe the blade has missed the major organs and vessels, but as we remove it we may reveal a bleed that has been plugged by the knife, or there could be damage to the bowel underneath.'

'Is there anything we can do to decrease the risk?' Simon asked, his face pale.

'You must stay completely still, Lady Westcroft. Even moving a fraction of an inch could be the difference between life and death.' The doctor looked between Simon and Alice. 'I will prepare the needle for stitching the wound after. It will be painful, but I have laudanum in my bag which should ease you.'

'I do not want laudanum,' Alice said, thinking back to when she had hit the tree as a girl on horseback and bruised her ribs. The doctor then had given her laudanum, and she had fought terrible hallucinations for days. The alternative was significant pain whilst her wound was stitched, but she would take that over the painkiller any day.

'Very well.'

The doctor moved away and spoke to Miss Stick in a low voice, instructing her on all the things he would need. Simon returned to Alice's side, crouching down by the bed and holding her hand.

'You are brave, my sweet,' he said, lowering his lips to her hand and kissing the skin.

'I do not think I have a choice,' Alice replied with a weak smile. 'It was that man, Simon, that horrible man we saw with the gang of pickpockets.'

'He targeted you on purpose?'

'I think he was waiting for me outside the orphanage. He held the knife to me, in between my body and his so Drummond and Smith could not see it, and he was demanding my valuables, but I did not take anything with me. He asked for my wedding ring, and I was going to give it to him, but Drummond grew suspicious as to why it was taking me so long to cross to the carriage, and he and Smith rushed over. He grabbed my ring.' Alice looked down at her fingers where the ring had been, tears pooling in her eyes. 'Then he pushed past me and ran away. He must have lashed out with the knife when he pushed past me.'

'Do not worry about any of that now,' Simon said, stroking her hair from her face. 'Let us focus on getting you better, and then we can worry about the scoundrel who did this to you.'

The doctor returned to the bedside, a small tray of items in his hand. Alice glanced down at it and then wished she hadn't. There was a long needle on it, thick thread trailing from behind, as well as a couple of small knives and a pair of scissors. Thankfully Miss Stick returned at the same time, and Alice forced herself to watch the housekeeper's preparations rather than the doctor's.

'Are you ready, Lady Westcroft?'

'I am,' Alice said, taking a deep breath and closing her eyes. She tried to think of all the things that made her happy. The dappled sun through the trees in the park, the sound of the sea crashing against the dunes in Bamburgh on stormy nights, the giggles of her nieces and, of course, Simon.

He held her hand firmly as the doctor anchored the skin around the knife and then in a smooth, slow motion pulled it out.

Alice let out a low, wounded cry and then against her better judgement looked down at the wound.

Fresh blood welled out of the gash in her side, and she felt the room spin around her. Darkness pulled at the periphery of her vision, and she gripped Simon's hand harder, but she was unable to cling to consciousness.

Alice woke to pain much worse than what she had already endured. The doctor was leaned over her, piercing her skin with the needle. That hurt in itself, but even worse was the pain as he pulled the thread through after. She felt every inch slide through the fresh hole in her skin.

'You must stay still, Lady Westcroft,' Dr Black said, his voice authoritative. He turned to Simon and instructed, 'Keep her still.'

Alice felt Simon stand and lean over her, kissing her on her forehead. 'Stay still, Alice. You are doing very well. This will not take long, and then you can rest.'

She clenched her teeth and endured the pain, tears rolling down her cheeks, and it was a great relief when the doctor stepped away.

'She must rest. The knife was small, but unfortunately it was not clean. I worry the wound might fester.' The doctor glanced over at her, pity in his eyes. 'If she does develop a fever, then send for me. Otherwise I will call tomorrow to check on the wound.'

'Thank you, Dr Black,' Simon said, shaking the man's hand.

Simon approached the bed with trepidation. Miss Stick had tried to shoo him out of the room whilst she and one of the maids changed the bloodstained sheets around Alice, as deftly as they could without jostling her. He had acknowledged he was in the way but had felt unable to retreat farther than the chair in the corner of the room whilst they worked. Now they were finished, he pulled his chair closer to the bed and took Alice's hand in his.

Her eyes flickered open, and she gave him a weak smile, but her face was ashen, and underneath her eyes were dark circles. She looked terribly unwell.

Gently he kissed her fingers where they entwined with his and then sat back in the chair and waited.

Alice slept fitfully, every so often trying to turn in her sleep to get into a more comfortable position. When this happened he would spring forward and press her shoulders gently, holding her on her back so she did not pull at the stitches or disturb the wound.

'Please do not die,' he whispered time and time again. It was strange to be sitting here next to his young and normally healthy wife. A year ago he had been convinced Alice would outlive him, but here he was the picture of health and she was suspended in that awful void between life and death.

Periodically Miss Stick would knock quietly at the door and enter the room, taking her time to straighten the sheets and ensure Alice was comfortable. He saw real affection and concern in the housekeeper's eyes. In her short time in London, Alice had made an impression on so many people.

The housekeeper would also bring Simon trays of tea and press him to drink and eat a little, pouring out the tea and handing it to him, not leaving the room until he had taken at least a few sips.

The hours seemed to drag as Simon found he could not rest, not whilst Alice's future was so uncertain. Every so often he would place a hand on her brow, dreading he would feel the heat that would indicate the wound was infected, pus accumulating under the stitches.

It was dark outside when he finally nodded off to sleep, dozing fitfully in the armchair, waking every few minutes to glance across at Alice and then his head dropping down onto his chest.

Miss Stick offered to sit with Alice so he could sleep, but Simon had an irrational fear that if he moved, if he left her bedside, something terrible would happen. He knew it was not true, but he could not help feeling that way.

As the first rays of sunshine filtered through the gap in the curtains, Alice stirred, her eyes flickering open as they had through the night, but this time she seemed to focus on him.

'How are you, my love?'

She smiled at him weakly and tried to push herself up in bed. Simon laid a restraining hand on her arm.

'Everything hurts,' she said, her face contorting into a frown.

'I can send for the doctor if you would like some opium, or perhaps just the laudanum he offered you yesterday.'

'No,' Alice said quickly. 'I just need to change position. Will you help me?'

'Of course.'

She was light and easy to manoeuvre, and slowly they managed to get her sitting up a little more. He regarded her with a frown. She was still terribly pale, but it was good to see her alert and able to focus on him.

'I am awfully thirsty.'

'Would you like water? Tea?'

'Just some water.' He poured her a glass from the jug in the corner of the room and held it to her lips as she took small sips. 'Have you been here all night?'

'Yes.'

'That is kind. Thank you.'

'I could not have been anywhere else,' he said, hearing the anguish in his own voice. He didn't want to examine what it meant. He didn't want to acknowledge the deep panic he felt at the idea of losing Alice. It was as though she had buried into his heart and become part of him.

'I feel better knowing you are here,' Alice said as she closed her eyes and drifted off to sleep again.

Chapter Nineteen

Alice spent an entire week in bed, and by the end she could quite happily have never seen another pillow or bed-sheet again in her life. Around day two the wound on her abdomen had reddened and grown tight, pulling at the stitches. Dr Black had visited, a grave expression on his face, asking to speak to Simon privately after he had examined the wound. Later Simon had told her of the doctor's concerns of infection and that if the redness and swelling did not settle, he might have to snip the stitches to let the accumulated pus out.

Thankfully the swelling had not worsened and after another day began to subside, and Alice did not succumb to a fever as they feared she might.

Dr Black was cautious and had insisted she stay in bed for the whole week, but today was her first day of freedom.

'I see that glint in your eyes,' Simon said, shaking his head. 'Do not think you are going to be running around this house just because you have been given permission to get out of bed.'

'If I stay in this room one day longer, I think I will go mad.'

'Dr Black said you could get up and sit in the chair, not go charging round the house like an excitable dog who has not seen his master for days.'

Alice sighed. She had hoped to make it downstairs. It would be wonderful to sit in the drawing room, perhaps in a chair by the window as she watched people on the street outside go about their lives.

'Let me help you,' he said, and he leaned down so Alice could slip an arm around his neck. He lifted her smoothly and then helped her to gently set her feet on the ground.

It felt strange to be standing again, and for a moment Alice's legs felt weak and wobbly, but Simon was there, as he had been this entire past week. Not once had he left her alone for more than an hour, using the time when she slept to bathe and change clothes and conduct the urgent bits of business that could not wait.

She had grown used to his constant attention, and his presence had made a difficult week much more bearable. They had read together, he had taught her to play chess, he had told her of his childhood, of the happy memories with his parents and his brother, and she had shared more of what her life had been like growing up in Bamburgh. She had thought at some point he would pull away, especially when it became more and more certain that she would make a full recovery, his duty done. Yet he had not. Each morning he was there in the chair beside her bed, and each evening he leaned over to kiss her, passion bubbling under the surface, barely restrained.

It was a stark contrast to the week they had spent prior to Alice's injury, unable to keep their hands from one another. Yet despite her injury Alice found she had enjoyed this second week together almost as much. She had a deeper understanding of her husband now, and she felt he had truly relaxed around her.

He settled her into the chair they had positioned by the window and took a seat beside her then closed his eyes and let out a jagged sigh.

'Is something amiss, Simon?'

He shook his head, but for a moment he did not look at her.

'You do not know how worried I have been,' he said quietly. 'When I saw you with that knife sticking out of you…' He shook his head.

'I know,' Alice said, biting her lip at the memory of the panic she had felt when she had looked down and seen the knife in her for the first time.

'I thought you were going to die. People who get stabbed do not often survive, especially if they are stabbed in the abdomen.'

'I am lucky, I know that.' She reached out and gripped his hand, waiting until he looked at her to continue. 'But the worst is over. Dr Black said so. The wound is healing well, and in a few days he will come and remove the stitches. I will have to avoid heavy lifting and strenuous activity for a while, but it will not be for ever.'

'I know you are recovering well, Alice,' Simon said. 'And I am so grateful for your strength.' He fell silent again.

Alice opened her mouth to speak, trying to find the right words to gently prompt to see if the issue were how their relationship had changed again. In the few weeks since his return, they had moved quickly from tiptoeing around each other to friendship and then being unable to keep their hands off one another. This past week had been another change again, with Simon caring for her as any true husband would care for his wife.

She felt a flicker of hope and wondered if this last week had made him realise what was important in his life. Not for the first time her mind started to fire pictures of their perfect future together at her. She imagined them strolling hand and hand through London before spending a few hours together raising money and awareness for the orphanage. Then at the end of the day they would return home together to retire to the bedroom and enjoy one another's company in a more intimate way. She even dared to dream of children, a little baby of their own, a house filled with happiness and love.

Alice hadn't even dared to dream about such a future, but Simon had changed this week. He had stopped trying to hold her at a distance and instead allowed her to see every part of him.

Before Alice could find the right words to ask if perhaps his feelings towards her and their future had changed, there was a gentle knock on the door, and a moment later Miss Stick entered.

'You have a visitor, Lady Westcroft.'

Simon frowned. They had kept visitors away this past week so she could focus on recovery, but the room was filled with flowers from well-wishers. Miss Stick had been wonderful at gently guiding friends and acquaintances away, suggesting they visit in a week or two when Alice was back on her feet.

'Hardly a visitor,' Maria said as she burst into the room. 'My darling Alice, I came the very second I heard the news. Let me look at you.' Maria swept over and knelt before Alice, regarding her carefully, then laid a hand on her heart and let out a choked sob. 'You're going to recover,' she said, tears dropping onto her cheeks. 'Forgive me, but for the entire journey here I feared you would have succumbed to infection, and I would be arriving to a house in mourning.'

Alice gripped Maria's hands, wishing she could pull her into an embrace but wary of the strain on her stitches.

Maria stood, turning to Simon and hugged him. 'You must be so relieved.'

'It has been a worrying week,' he admitted.

'But I am well on my way to recovery now. The doctor insisted I stay in bed for a whole week, but today, finally, I have been allowed up.'

'Sit down, Maria,' Simon said, indicating the chair next to Alice's. 'I will arrange some refreshment. You must be thirsty.'

'I am famished too. The coach set off before breakfast this morning, and in my rush to get here I have not stopped for it since.'

'I will organise food and tea.'

Simon strolled out of the room as Maria settled in the chair. Alice felt a great happiness at having her sister-in-law here. Out of everyone from her old family and new, Maria was the one she had leaned on the most this past year.

'You must tell me everything that happened. How did you get such an injury? Was it through your work with the orphanages?'

'Indirectly. I was visiting one of them near St Giles, and a man tried to rob me. He wanted my wedding ring, and as I was trying to take it off my finger, the driver and footman who had accompanied me realised some-thing was wrong. They rushed over, and in the thief's desperation to get away he stabbed me.'

Maria's hand went to her mouth. 'You must have been so frightened, Alice.'

'It didn't feel real, not until we were back here and the doctor was talking about pulling the knife out and stitching me up.'

'The wound is healing? It has not festered?'

'No. There was a day or two where we thought it might go that way, but thankfully the redness subsided and it has since healed well.'

Maria leaned forward in her chair and lowered her voice. 'And what of Simon? I didn't expect the look of devotion he was giving you when I first arrived.'

'Simon has been wonderful,' Alice said carefully. She knew how invested Maria was in her brother-in-law's happiness and how much she wanted him to settle down and allow himself to experience the same sort of wed-ded bliss she had found with Robert. 'He has barely left my side.'

'He was always a kind boy, sensitive too, although that is hidden underneath the layers of grief and the hard shell of an exterior he has to project in his role as earl.'

'He is kind,' Alice said softly. He was so much more than that. She thought of the way he had kept her enter-tained during her recovery, which was wonderful in it-self, but she knew he had done it to ensure her the best possible chance of getting better. If her mind was stim-ulated and he did not allow her to grow bored, then she was more likely to follow the doctor's orders and stay in bed.

'You have not found it too difficult, having him back?'

'I cannot lie. It was a shock at first, but I think we have found a happy equilibrium together.' She bit her lip, wondering what their relationship would look like when she was fully recovered. Her injury had put a stop to the physical intimacy they had shared in the week before she was stabbed, but their relationship had not faltered as she had been worried it might. Instead it had flourished.

'He has not mentioned leaving again?'

'No.' Alice felt her heart squeeze at the thought. She had told herself she would not become too used to Simon's company, but she knew if he left now she would be devastated. These past few weeks, she had tried her hardest to remember he did not want a deeper relationship, but slowly and surely she had fallen in love with her husband.

She pressed her lips together and glanced over her shoulder, wondering if she should confide in Maria, but before she could say anything Simon walked back into the room.

'Tea and toast and cake will be brought up shortly,' he said.

'Perhaps you might carry me downstairs, Simon. There is more room in the drawing room, and I would like a change of scenery.'

He considered for a moment and then nodded. 'If you are sure. Just for half an hour, though, then I will carry you back up to bed.'

Alice didn't argue, excited by the prospect of leaving her room for the first time in a week. Carefully Simon leaned down and positioned his arms underneath her, lifting her up smoothly from the chair. He walked slowly, ensuring his footsteps did not jar or jolt Alice as she held onto his neck.

They made it downstairs without incident, and Simon settled Alice in a comfortable armchair, ensuring she had just the right number of pillows behind her.

'Thank you,' Alice said, beaming up at him.

'You're welcome.' He dropped a kiss on the top of her head and then moved away. 'I will tell Miss Stick to take the opportunity to change your sheets now you are out of bed. I am sure it will feel good to have fresh ones.' He disappeared, and once again Alice was left alone with Maria.

Maria stared after him and then rose from her seat and softly closed the door behind her.

'Is something amiss?' Alice asked, confused at their need for privacy.

'You're in love with him,' Maria said, her eyes wide. 'It is obvious with every look, every touch.'

Alice started to shake her head and then stopped. It was impossible to hide such things from Maria: she was astute in all areas, but in particular she had a very well-developed emotional intelligence.

'We have grown close these last few weeks.'

'I can see that,' Maria said, studying Alice carefully. 'You have forgiven him for abandoning you?'

'Yes.'

Maria looked at Alice cautiously, as if aware her next question was delicate, especially for a woman who was up for the first time in days and shouldn't be upset.

'Have you spoken of your future together? Has he said he wants to settle down with you?'

'We have spoken many times,' Alice said, shaking

her head a little, recalling their conversations in Hyde Park and later in the carriage and the again in the bedroom. Each had resulted in a different plan, a different conclusion. 'But we have agreed on nothing long-term.'

'I do not wish you to get hurt, Alice.'

'I know. I do not wish for that either.' She lowered her voice further so it was barely more than a whisper. 'I have tried my very hardest not to fall in love with Simon these last few weeks, but I fear I have been unsuccessful. At first I tried to keep my distance, and then I told myself we could be close just as long as I remembered not to fall for him. I was very resolute at first, but he has a way of burrowing into your heart.'

'He is very loveable,' Maria said with a sigh. 'But so are you, and you deserve to be loved, Alice.'

'I cannot force him to love me,' she said quietly, wondering if she was mad to think that perhaps he did love her. Over the past week he had certainly been devoted to her care and recovery, and every time he came into the room he smiled broadly, a smile that told her he was pleased to see her. She thought maybe he did love her: he was just too stubborn to admit it, still ruled by the guilt of taking over every aspect of his late brother's life.

'He is a fool,' Maria said suddenly, anger flaring in her voice. 'I love you both dearly, but until I saw him with you today, I could not imagine how you would be together, yet you are perfect, you complement each other in exactly the right ways. It is an incredible turn of events, marrying a stranger and ending up with the one person you are destined for in this life, and if he squanders this chance of happiness, he is a complete and utter fool.'

'I think the problem is he feels he shouldn't be happy.'

'Silly boy,' Maria said, biting her lip and shaking her head at the same time. 'Do you want me to talk to him?'

'No,' Alice said quickly. She needed to step carefully with Simon; the last thing she wanted was to push him away. If he was made to confront his feelings for Alice too soon it might scare him away. It would be better to let things build, for him to see there was no point denying the love and happiness they brought to one another.

'If you are sure?'

'I am sure.'

'You two look deadly serious,' Simon said as he re-entered the room.

'We were discussing Alice's injury. It sounds horrific,' Maria turned to Alice and leaned over and squeezed her hand. 'You should return to Northumberland, where it is safe, as soon as you are well.'

Alice smiled. Maria had a motherly, protective instinct that sometimes went a little too far, but it came from a place of affection and love.

'I hardly think Alice need quit London for good,' Simon said quickly, 'just avoid certain areas.'

'I can't stay away from St Benedict's Orphanage for ever. The London Ladies' Benevolent Society has great plans for that place.'

'You are incorrigible,' Simon muttered. 'You were stabbed outside its doors, and still you will not give it up.'

'It is a worthy cause.'

Simon shrugged. 'I am going to invoke my privilege as husband and insist you do not go there ever again unless I am by your side.'

'I will agree without argument, as long as you make yourself available to me whenever I wish to visit.'

'I can see no problem with that,' Simon said softly.

* * *

Two hours later Alice was back in bed, resting. She had not wanted to admit she was fatigued by the short spell she had spent downstairs, but as Simon had carried her back up to the bedroom she had leaned in close to him and nuzzled her face into his neck.

'Was it too much for you, my dear?'

'No,' Alice said quickly, 'just enough. I am a little tired now, but I enjoyed seeing a different view of these four walls.'

Simon helped her to get comfortable in bed and then made to sit in the chair next to her.

'You should spend some time with Maria,' Alice said, trying to stifle a yawn. 'It will do you good to get some fresh air, and I can hardly accompany you out anytime soon.'

'What if you need anything?'

'I am sure Miss Stick will be more than happy to check on me at regular intervals, and I have a loud voice to call out if I need something desperately.'

A day ago he would have dismissed the idea immediately, but Alice's strength was returning quickly now, and he realised it would be good to get outside and enjoy some fresh air.

'If you are sure?'

'I am. In fact, I insist.'

Half an hour later he and Maria were on horseback, riding side by side towards the park. Maria was an excellent rider, confident and at ease around the horse he had chosen for her, even though she had never ridden it before. It made Simon think back to the pleasant ride he had shared with Alice a few weeks earlier. They had still been feeling their way through their relationship at that point, wondering if they could even live companionably in the same part of the country. Now the idea of living apart from her made him feel a little sick.

'Thank you for coming down. I know Alice enjoys your company immensely.'

'I packed my bags as soon as I received the news she had been hurt.' Maria paused before continuing mildly, not looking at him. 'I was worried she would be gravely wounded with no one who cared about her to look after her.'

'I am here,' Simon said quietly. He had known Maria a long time and knew she wasn't lashing out to hurt him and would get to her true point soon.

'Yes, you are, but when I last saw you we spoke of your wife who you had left in London after not bidding her farewell. You told me you did not know what you planned to do with her, but that you would try to accommodate her wishes, unless of course she wished to have a true and full marriage with you.'

'I was young and naïve.'

'It was four weeks ago, Simon.'

'A lot has happened in four weeks.'

'Evidently. I rush down here thinking Alice might be all alone, and I find you devoted to her comfort, the very picture of a loving husband.'

'Would you rather I abandoned her?'

'Good Lord, no. This is exactly what I have always hoped for you. Marriage is a wonderful gift if done right, and I think with Alice you have the chance to build something truly special.'

He remained silent. It was difficult to deny the feelings that had grown inside him over the past few weeks. He had always felt an attraction to Alice, but the more time he spent with her the more he realised he liked her too. She was kind and generous and entertaining to converse with. She had an opinion on most matters of politics or social dilemmas. Added to that was her natural warmth, the way she could get virtual strangers to trust her, to feel like treasured confidants.

'I do not know *exactly* what I feel for her,' Simon said, acknowledging how difficult this was for him. He had enjoyed the time spent in Alice's company, but with it had come guilt. Guilt that he was happy, living his life, whilst Robert was long gone.

'Perhaps you don't need to know. Perhaps it is enough to realise you make one another happier together than you are apart.'

Simon looked down at the reins in his hands, glad that there was the distraction of riding that meant he did not have to look Maria directly in the eye as they spoke.

'I cannot just banish what I feel about Robert,' he said eventually.

'I know. I doubt it will ever leave you completely, Simon, but you knew Robert better than anyone else. He loved you so much, and he wanted you to be happy. That would never have changed, and I know if he is looking down on us now he will be shouting for you to stop being so pigheaded and stubborn, to stop using his death as an excuse not to live your own life.'

'He was the best of brothers.'

'He was, and we were lucky enough to have time with him in this world.' Maria reached across the gap between them and grasped his wrist, waiting until he looked at her to continue. 'Honour his memory in the way he would have wanted it. Live your life as he would, being fair and kind and conscientious. Love with all your heart. That is a greater tribute to Robert than hiding away and never allowing yourself any happiness.'

For a long time they rode in silence, Maria content to sit quietly in her saddle to give Simon the space to think on what she had said. He knew in many ways Maria was right. Robert had only ever been thoughtful and generous; he would not begrudge Simon any happiness. The feeling of guilt—that he was stealing the life Robert should have had—had come directly from himself. It was a conviction that was difficult to shake.

Yet here he was considering an alternative. As they rode through the park Simon allowed himself to imagine what his life could be. Waking up to the woman he loved, taking long, leisurely strolls whilst they discussed anything from their families to what the latest law to pass in Parliament meant for the wider country. Then home to tumble into bed together. It was an enthralling glimpse into what the future could be.

'Lord Lathum and his wife have just had a baby,' Maria said suddenly.

Simon was pulled back to the present and looked at his sister-in-law in confusion. He barely knew Lord and Lady Lathum.

'I am pleased for them.'

'They are healthy. She is not yet eighteen, chosen for her childbearing potential and sizeable dowry, I am told,' Maria said, turning her horse around so they could start the walk back to the house. 'He is your age, certainly no older. There have been no problems in the family previously, but their child has been born with an unnaturally large head and an extra finger on his left hand.'

Simon blinked, wondering what point she was trying to make.

'You have lost me, Maria,' he said eventually.

'Let me speak plainly.'

'Please do,' he murmured.

Maria pressed on, ignoring him. 'I am hopeful that in the course of the next few weeks you will see the only sensible thing to do is to commit to a full and happy marriage with the sweet young woman you decided to marry last year. You will be blissfully happy, but for your wife at least there will be one thing missing from your union.'

'Children,' he said, his face darkening. He knew how much Alice loved children. She spoke of their nieces with such affection, and every time they passed a young child with their nanny or nursemaid in the street, her eyes lit up. She had a patient and caring nature, and instinctively Simon knew his wife would make a wonderful mother.

'Yes, children. Alice has never come out and said she wishes a house filled to the brim with children, but I can see it in her eyes.'

'That is one thing I will not be persuaded to change my mind on.'

'Lord and Lady Lathum should have had a healthy child. The odds were in their favour, yet they are devastated their firstborn son has not been born healthy.'

'I do not get your point, Maria,' Simon snapped.

Luckily Maria did not offend easily, and she ignored his abrupt tone.

'None of us know what the future may hold.'

'That is exactly what Alice says.'

'You may drop dead tomorrow or you might live until you are a crotchety old man of ninety. Take Alice as a wonderful example. She is young and healthy, but if that knife had been thrust in with a fraction more force or an inch higher, it would have hit her liver, and Alice would have bled out on the streets of St Giles.'

Simon grimaced.

'I have said enough,' Maria said and nodded in grim satisfaction. 'I know you do not wish to discuss it with me, but I owe it to Alice to at least try. I love her like a sister, and I would hate for her to find happiness with you only to realise that very happiness was stopping her from having the family she dreamed of.'

'It isn't as if she can choose not to be married to me. She cannot suddenly decide to go and make a future with another man, a man who does wish to have children.'

'Of course she can,' Maria said, shaking her head. 'Perhaps not within the social circles we move in, but there are plenty of women who reside with a man who is not their husband, someone who provides a home for them, love, children.'

'You go too far, Maria,' he said wearily. 'Alice would not do that.'

'No, she wouldn't,' his sister-in-law said quietly. 'You are right, but perhaps it serves to remind you that in saying you will never have children, you are also saying she will never have children. *You* are making a significant decision about Alice's future and expecting her to accept it without discussion.'

'We have discussed it.'

'Telling her you will never father a child and discussing the issue are not the same, Simon,' she chastised gently.

'I need some time to think,' Simon said, aware he sounded unforgivably rude, but his head was spinning, and he had the sudden urge to be alone. He needed time to work through everything Maria had said to him. The last thing he wanted was to make Alice unhappy.

'Of course. I will return home and check on Alice. You take all the time you need.'

It was almost dark by the time Simon dismounted outside the townhouse, handing Socrates's reins to the groom and looking up at the window of the room where Alice was recuperating. He was eager to return to her side. For the past week they had spent hardly any time apart, but he knew he would have to hold his tongue and perhaps even lie to her about what he and Maria had discussed that afternoon.

On his ride through Hyde Park after Maria had left him, he had turned over their conversation, examining it from each possible angle, until his head had started to throb. He had been unable to concentrate, so he had dismounted and sat on a bench overlooking the lake, trying to think of nothing but the ripples on the water in front of him.

As he sat, he had come to a realisation, one that he wished to share with Alice, but he knew she was not up to it yet. It might be weeks before she was strong enough to hear what he had to say, and the last thing he wanted to do was set her recovery back by any degree.

'I missed you,' Alice said as he knocked on the door and entered. Maria had been sitting by the bed, but she rose when Simon entered and murmured an excuse to go. Simon caught her by the hand as she walked past him, and Maria paused.

He smiled at her, squeezing her hand gently, and she searched his eyes for the answer to an unspoken question, and then she reached out and embraced him. Maria was the only person who could speak to him so freely and he would forgive in a heartbeat.

When they were alone, Alice looked at him curiously. 'What was that about?'

'Whilst we were out, Maria reminded me what a fool I was being.'

'A fool?'

'Yes.' He leaned down and kissed Alice on the forehead. 'It does not matter, my sweet. You rest, and I will tell you everything when you are recovered.'

Chapter Twenty

Three weeks later Alice stepped out of the door for the first time in a month. Her stitches had been removed by Dr Black, and she was declared fit to start building up to her normal levels of activity. To her dismay she had lost some muscle whilst invalided, and she knew it would not be an easy feat to get back to rushing around London, attending to her various commitments.

Alice was determined to make a good start and today had suggested she and Simon step out for a short walk around the local streets. It was early, only a little past nine o'clock in the morning. Alice had chosen this time deliberately for two reasons. The first was to avoid the jostling of people walking on the pavements later in the day. At nine o'clock most wealthy people were still at breakfast or readying themselves for the day, so the streets around Grosvenor Square were quiet. The second reason was that she did not wish to encounter any of her friends and acquaintances when she left the house for the first time. She was excited to get back to normal, but she did not particularly want to stop to reassure people she was recovering well multiple times on her walk.

'Are you ready?'

She breathed in deeply and then nodded. 'I am ready.'

'You will tell me if you start to tire?'

'I promise.'

They set off at a sedate pace, walking as you would if accompanying an elderly relative out and about, but after she had got used to moving outside again, Alice found she did not mind ambling along. She was pleasantly surprised to find her wound did not pull too much when she walked. Dr Black was right: the skin had knitted together beautifully, leaving her with a neat scar that he assured her would get smaller with time.

Simon was quiet as they walked ,and Alice wondered what he was thinking. He had been attentive these last few weeks, but sometimes she thought he was distracted, staring off into the distance for some time before focussing his attention in the room again. Once or twice she had panicked that he might be thinking about leaving again, finally fed up of life in London, life with her. Quickly she had pushed away the thought. Alice was trying to enjoy what time they did share and not think too much on the future, despite wishing Simon would fall to his knees, declare himself a fool and tell her he had loved her since their very first kiss.

They turned at the corner, planning on doing a small loop around the local streets before ending up back home. As they crossed the road to start on the second side of the square, a man in the distance called out.

Alice was horrified to find she stiffened, unable to move for a second. It was her first time out since the attack, and although physically she was more than ready, she did feel a little apprehensive.

The man in the distance called again, waving jovially.

'Northumberland,' the person shouted, taking his hat from his head and waving it.

'I take it you know that man?'

Simon frowned, looking hard at the man before shaking his head. 'It sounds like I should know him, but I do not recognise him.'

'He's coming over. Perhaps he will introduce himself to me.'

The man approached quickly, and then when he was five feet away he stood stock-still and looked at Simon strangely.

'My apologies, sir. I thought you were someone else.'

'We do not know each other?' Simon asked.

'No. I thought you were the Earl of Northumberland, an old friend of mine.'

'I am the earl,' Simon said, his voice dropping low.

'The Earl of Northumberland?'

'Yes. You must have known my father or my brother.'

'I knew Robert,' the man said, looking a little uncomfortable.

'My brother. He died a few years ago.'

'My deepest condolences. I apologise profusely for the misunderstanding. I have been out of the country some time, and I had not heard about your brother's death. You are very much like him in looks and countenance.'

Alice sucked in a sharp breath as she felt Simon sway almost imperceptibly beside her. She wanted to pull Simon away, to stop him from hearing the man's words. She knew he found it difficult to hear how similar he was to Robert. It brought to the fore the feelings that he had stepped into his brother's life, replacing him in every way.

'It is an easy mistake to make,' Simon said, nodding to the man before turning away.

'We can return home,' Alice suggested as they began to put space between them and the man.

'There is no need. I am perfectly fine.'

'It was an unsettling encounter. It is not weakness to admit you are a little upset.'

'I am not upset, I am not unsettled. I told you I am fine.'

Alice fell silent. Her husband was far from fine, no matter what he told her. He started walking a little quicker now, his head bent and his eyes darting from side to side. At first Alice tried to keep up, but as they walked faster the movement pulled at her scar, and after a couple of minutes she slipped her arm from his and stopped. Simon did not notice, at least not for a good few seconds, and when he did finally look up and around, it was with an air of barely suppressed irritation.

When he spotted her, he returned quickly.

'I think I want to return home,' she said, looking back over her shoulder at the way they had come.

'Of course.' He offered her his arm, but Alice waved it away, plastering a wide smile on her face. 'I am fine, Simon. I will walk home by myself. I am sure you have other things to do.'

For a moment she thought he would brush off her suggestion and escort her home, and they would return to their normal routine of the last few weeks, but instead he nodded, turning absently away from her.

Alice felt her heart squeeze and then shatter. Everything had been going so well, and then with one reminder of the brother whose place he had taken, Simon had completely regressed. Of course she did not mind if he showed emotion, if he leaned in and told her how difficult it was when he was mistaken for the brother he had loved so much: they could have shared that sadness. But instead he had blocked her out completely.

Quickly she turned, walking away before Simon could see how distressed she was.

The footman opened the door, surprise on his face that she had returned alone. Alice hurried in and struggled up the stairs to her room, forcing herself to remain calm. Simon had been upset, that was all, and she did not begrudge him some space to work through the emotions he felt at being mistaken for his brother. She would rather he talked to her about it, but she could not force that.

'Be calm,' she told herself, resisting the urge to pace over to the window and see if Simon had changed his mind and was returning.

For hours Simon walked, without sparing a thought for where he would end up or what direction he was travelling in. He thought he knew London well, but the streets passed in a blur, with the buildings getting smaller and closer together as he moved farther away from the centre of London to the poorer outskirts. At some point early on he must have crossed over the river, for when he stopped walking hours later he was well south of the Thames, but he did not have any recollection of doing so.

It was the fading light and lengthening shadows that brought him back to his senses. For a long time he had walked, head bent, trying to gain control of all the awful thoughts running through his mind, but he felt completely overwhelmed.

He took a moment to look around him, feeling as

though he had just come out of a trance. He was out of
the city proper, the roads widening and only a few scattered houses on either side. Vaguely he recalled travelling by this road on a few occasions: it was one of the few
that led out of London to the south, the route travellers
to Sussex would take to start their journey to the coast.

Now he had stopped he was aware of the ache in his
legs and feet. He was an active man, often walking for
hours in the Tuscan hills in the last year and enjoying
long, physically challenging rides on horseback as well,
but he realised he must have been walking for at least six
or seven hours. His mouth was dry, and he longed for
something to quench his thirst. In the distance he could
see the smartly painted swinging sign for one of the inns
that were dotted along the main routes out of London to
provide shelter and refreshments for weary travellers.

It only took him a couple of minutes to make his way
to the inn where he was welcomed by a middle-aged
woman with a smile and the offer of ale. He ordered and
was thankful when the drink arrived, downing half the
tankard as soon as he raised it to his lips.

Thankfully the inn was quiet, and Simon had found
a corner table to himself so he was able to nurse the rest
of the ale in peace, undisturbed by the few other patrons.

After a moment he closed his eyes, feeling awfully
weary. He could not quite believe he had been walking
for so long.

'Alice,' he murmured, thinking of how he had just
abandoned her in the middle of the street when he was
meant to be escorting her. It was inexcusable, yet he had
been unable to act in any other way. When the man had
approached them, mistaking Simon for his brother, he

had felt as though he had been shot through the heart. Every day he woke up wishing his brother were alive, feeling guilty that he got to continue with life when Robert did not. Ever since his talk with Maria, he had spent each day fighting so hard to push the feeling away, to convince himself he was something more than an imposter living the life his brother should have had. Then the feeling had come rushing back in an instant with one innocent little mistake.

For a minute Simon cradled his head in his hands, trying to unpick the tangled web of thoughts and mess of emotions jumbled inside him. It had been one of the reasons he had walked for so long: as soon as he stopped, the sorrow and despair threatened to overwhelm him, but he knew the answer wasn't running for ever.

He took another large gulp of ale and motioned for the barmaid to bring another over. He would only have the one more—the last thing he needed was to lose control of his senses.

Simon sat back in his chair and watched the other people in the room for a moment and then drained the last of the ale from his tankard. He knew he had to let his thoughts in, to acknowledge the pain he was feeling, the doubts, but part of him wanted to keep pushing it away.

'Here you are, sir,' the barmaid said, placing the ale down in front of him. 'Anything else I can get you?'

'No, thank you.' He tried to empty his mind as he stared into the full tankard of ale, but his thoughts were still racing. These last few weeks he had been pretending everything was all right, that he wasn't about to fall apart any moment. He had felt real happiness with

Alice, a sense of contentment that he now feared he did not deserve.

His mind brought forward an image that he often saw in those quiet moments when nothing else was happening. It was of Robert and Maria at their wedding, coming out of the church with their heads bent together. The image was as clear to Simon as if he were looking at a painting, even down to the blissful expressions on their faces.

He'd felt that same bliss when he'd been walking arm-in-arm with Alice, that same contentment. In his mind he had been planning what their future might be like, pushing aside the doubts that plagued him about how long he would live.

Deep in his chest he felt a throb of pain. For the last few weeks he had been lying to himself, pretending he was worthy of something he was not. If he pursued a relationship with Alice, he would be seeking that same happiness his brother had enjoyed, that same ideal of family life. If he followed his heart, he would be stepping into Robert's shoes completely, choosing a contented, domestic life.

'I can't be you,' he murmured, low enough not to attract any attention. 'I can't take your life.'

Morosely Simon stared into his ale, not knowing what was for the best. He couldn't just abandon Alice—that would be cruel—but he didn't know what he wanted from his life. He could either pursue happiness and lead a life plagued by guilt or accept that he couldn't be with Alice, despite falling for her these last few weeks.

Twenty-four hours later Simon was not back, and Alice's mild concern had turned to devastation and anger.

After everything they had been through, he had left again, disappeared without a word. She understood the strong emotions he felt around inheriting his brother's title, and if he had been here in the house she would have given him space to work through how he was feeling.

The problem was he wasn't in the house. He hadn't even sent a note to let her know where he was or how long he was planning on being absent. He could be half-way to France by now or boarding a boat for any part of the world he desired. The last time he had felt overwhelmed, he'd run away, fleeing the country. She wasn't entirely convinced he wouldn't do the same this time.

'I will not stay here, perpetually waiting,' Alice murmured, and decisively she crossed to the corner of the room and pulled the bell cord to summon the maid.

A minute later she appeared at Alice's door, bobbing into a little curtsy. 'What can I do, my Lady?'

'Ask Miss Stick to have my trunk brought up to my room and to get Drummond to ready the carriage and the horses.'

'Yes, my Lady.'

Alice began pulling her dresses out and quickly started to fold them. She did not care that they would be creased in the trunk, she could have them steamed when she arrived in Northumberland. All she cared about was getting away from London and away from Simon.

'Alice, the maid said you were packing to leave,' Maria said as she came into the room.

'I am planning on returning to Northumberland immediately.'

Maria raised an eyebrow in question.

'He's gone, Maria. Yesterday when we were out walking, an old acquaintance of Robert's thought Simon was his older brother. It upset him, and he left almost immediately. I thought he would walk about for a while to think about things and then he would come home.'

'But he didn't return?'

Alice shook her head miserably. 'I have no idea where he is or if he is ever coming back.'

'Of course he is coming back, Alice. He loves you.'

'Does he? He has never told me so. He looks after me, treats me as an equal, but he has never been able to say that he loves me.'

Maria chewed on her lip. 'You are set on leaving?'

'I am, just as soon as I am packed.'

'Then, I will come with you. It would not be right for you to travel on your own after such an injury.'

'Are you sure?'

'Of course. I tire of London, especially as my girls are in Northumberland. I will return with you. Perhaps you can stay with me and the girls for a while. I do not think you should be on your own.'

'I would like that,' Alice said, suddenly feeling weary. She wanted to collapse on the bed and cry until she had no more tears to shed. She had allowed herself to believe Simon loved her, even if he could not bring himself to say it. She'd thought it was just because he found it difficult to acknowledge he was finally allowing himself to experience a little happiness.

'Come, Alice. I will make the arrangements. In a few days we will be back in Northumberland, and Simon will have to deal with an empty house here when he does emerge from wherever he has taken himself.'

Morosely Alice nodded and allowed herself to be cajoled and organised into getting everything she might possibly need for a summer spent in Northumberland.

Chapter Twenty-One

Simon climbed the last of the winding stairs, gripping the handrail as his foot struck the top one. He considered himself to be a fit and active man, yet even he was a little out of breath as he emerged into the cool late-afternoon air. It had been twenty years since he had last climbed the three hundred and eleven steps of the Monument, situated close to the magnificent St Paul's Cathedral. It had been one of his father's favourite places in London, and when he was young his father would often pay the entrance fee for him and Simon and then race his son up the stairs to the top. Once up there they would pick a spot on the narrow platform and stare out over London.

His father used to enjoy pointing out the magnificent buildings of the city, but for Simon it was the peace and the companionship he cherished the most. This was something that was his to share with his father, a sacred place where he could feel at peace.

Robert had offered to take him up the Monument once after their father had died, but Simon declined, wanting to keep his memories unsullied.

Now he stood alone, wishing his father and brother were by his side. There had been so much grief over the years, along with so much fear. It was hard to think about both. Despite his loving family, despite the best efforts of his mother and Maria, he had suppressed both his grief and his fear, pushing them deep down inside him where they had grown and got horribly out of control.

Up here, with the wind whipping at his face, he felt a moment of clarity after a difficult twenty-four hours. When he had been out walking with Alice and the man had called over to him, it had felt like his worst fear had come true, that someone had proved Simon had stolen Robert's life. Of course, now he looked at it rationally he could see that wasn't the case. It was merely an old acquaintance of his brother who had been momentarily confused by a family resemblance. Yet still he felt as though it had caused a monumental shift inside him, forcing him to confront his own fears and limitations. These last few weeks he had pushed aside his doubts about his happiness and his future, but they were still there, waiting to surface.

He closed his eyes, trying to empty his mind of everything but his doubts about the future, but as always it was the past that clung on, haunting him. The memory of his father came to him, but not the happy times, not the time spent exploring the countryside or strolling along the beach. Instead he was confronted by the terrible image of his father rising from his desk in his study, smiling as Simon hurried towards him, ready to impart some important fact about his day. Simon remembered how his father had stiffened, his face becoming a mask, then without any other warning he had dropped to the ground, dead before Simon could even utter a word.

Simon felt the sting of tears in his eyes. The moment of his father's death was crystal-clear in his mind: he could remember every expression, every miniscule movement, until there was nothing more. The period after was a blur, an overwhelming maelstrom of grief and shock that he had never properly recovered from.

Thoughts of his father's death led his mind to Alice and the panic he had felt when she had been stabbed. In the immediate aftermath, he had functioned by seeing to the practicalities, and as the days became weeks he suppressed the fear and desperation, trying to pretend the feelings weren't there. Yet he knew they bubbled under the surface, just waiting for an opportunity to get out. When he had seen the blood seeping through her dress he had felt a cold dread, a certainty that he would lose her just like he lost the other people most dear to him. The thought had plagued him for weeks, even as she recovered and it became clear she would not die from her wound.

'It is all such a mess,' he muttered to himself. He wished he were free to love without consequence, to live his life without fearing death but also in the shadow of the grief that had haunted him for years. He wanted to welcome in the love he felt for Alice, but he knew with that love there came the possibility she might one day be hurt, and one day he might lose her too.

'What would you do, Father?' Simon asked, gripping the railing. His father had always seemed so wise, contemplating Simon's questions and dilemmas with a serious demeanour, but always his answers would contain a little humour, something to show his son life was for enjoying as well as doing your duty.

He knew what his father would say. He could even

hear his deep, melodious voice as he urged Simon to live his life, to grab any chance at love, at happiness. Robert would tell him the same.

Simon felt the tears welling in his eyes. He did know how lucky he was to have been loved by two such incredible men. His father with his kindness and his patience, and Robert who had always been the sort of older brother everyone wished was their own.

He wondered how Robert would have coped if their lives were reversed, if Simon had been the one to die at a young age and Robert had survived. He knew the answer immediately. Robert would have gathered his family around him and ensured he made the most of every moment with his beautiful wife and children. He wouldn't have run away or spent his time wishing for things that could never be. He wouldn't have dwelt on questions he would never know the answer to or wasted his time worrying those he loved would be taken away.

'You have been a fool,' he murmured to himself, but even as he said the words he felt a flicker of rebellion inside him. For once he looked upon himself with kindness and compassion and reminded himself he had still been a boy when his father died, and although he was well into adulthood when Robert passed away, the sudden shock of his death would be enough to traumatise anyone.

Simon straightened, feeling a resolve like nothing he had experienced before. He knew it would not be a simple matter to start viewing himself with kindness, but he was going to try. There would be no more thoughts that he was less worthy than Robert, no more self-accusations that he was trying to step into his brother's life.

The first thing he had to do was make things right

with Alice. He had treated her terribly, unable to stop himself from showing her love and affection, but always holding back from telling her he loved her. It was cruel to keep her on edge and uncertain, and although that hadn't been his intention, it was no doubt the result. He could see now he had been holding part of himself back from her these last few weeks, not only because he felt guilty for feeling so happy but out of fear of giving his heart only to lose someone else he loved. It was understandable given his losses, but he hoped she could forgive him for pulling away when she needed him the most.

Taking in the view one last time, he turned and made his way back to the spiral staircase and then descended quickly, his feet clattering on the stone steps.

Back home the door was answered by a confused Frank Smith who looked at Simon as if he had grown an extra head.

'Where is Lady Westcroft?' Simon said, looking to the stairs and wondering if she was still resting from their trip out that had been cut short the day before.

'Lady Westcroft, my Lord?' Smith said, glancing over his shoulder.

'Yes, Smith. Where is my wife?'

'She left, my Lord. Her and the other Lady Westcroft.'

For a moment Simon could not move.

'Ah, you are home, my Lord,' Miss Stick said, emerging from the darkness of the stairs that led to the kitchen below. 'The Ladies Westcroft left a little earlier this morning. They took the carriage with Drummond and were heading for Northumberland.'

Simon reached out and steadied himself against

the wall. She'd gone. After everything he had put her through, she had finally had enough and left.

He did not blame her. He had behaved terribly yesterday, abandoning her when she was at such a low point. That would not be the worst part for Alice, though. Recently he had let her think that she could rely on him, and when she had started to trust he would not leave her again, he had disappeared without any regard for her.

'Will you pack for me, Miss Stick? I must follow my wife immediately. I will go and saddle Socrates.'

'Of course, my Lord.' Miss Stick hurried upstairs, and Simon made his way to the small stables. If he were quick, he would catch them on the road, although he would prefer privacy for what he needed to say to Alice.

It was a journey filled with peril and disaster. Only five miles out of London, Socrates threw a shoe. It was on a quiet stretch of road, a good mile out from the nearest village. Simon dismounted immediately and led Socrates by the reins to the village, hoping they had a farrier.

The farrier was able to fit Socrates with a new shoe, but the whole process took much longer than it should have. Simon wondered if the farrier was in league with the local tavern-keeper, for he delayed and delayed until it started to get dark, then suggested Simon rest Socrates overnight whilst he lodged in the tavern.

The next morning was no better with Simon coming upon an overturned carriage. The front wheel had splintered and flown off, and the carriage looked to have been dragged for some distance before the horses had been brought under control. Thankfully there were no fatalities, but one of the occupants, a young boy of eight, had fallen awkwardly on his arm, and the limb was bent at a strange angle.

Once he was satisfied no one else was badly injured, he put the boy on his horse and allowed him to ride to the next town where Simon sought out the local doctor and paid for his services. It meant he didn't begin his journey proper until after lunch and the distance he could cover before nightfall was limited.

When the third day of his journey dawned, he had only travelled fifty miles out of London and still had the prospect of many days ahead of him. It also meant the likelihood of catching up with Alice and Maria was very low, even though he could travel much quicker on horseback.

His third day of the journey was uneventful, but on the fourth disaster struck again as the inn where he was staying caught fire. He spent the morning stripped down to his shirtsleeves in a chain of men and women passing buckets of water from the river to throw on the blazing inn roof.

They were there for hours, and by the time the flames were under control the tavern had been decimated and half collapsed in on itself. Thankfully, due to the tireless efforts of everyone involved, the fire had not spread to any other buildings in the village.

Simon continued on his way much later that day, feeling as though his journey was cursed.

He arrived at Westcroft Hall in the early afternoon of a blustery, overcast day. There was a chance Alice had decided to go straight to one of the other properties he owned or to stay with Maria, but he felt she would have returned here first.

The door was opened by one of the young footmen who quickly took Simon's jacket and hat.

'Is my wife in residence?'

'She is, my Lord. She arrived yesterday.'

'Where is she?'

'I am here, Simon,' Alice said, her voice cool, with none of her usual affection.

He wanted to rush to her, to pull her into his arms and kiss her as if it were his last day on earth.

'I will ask Mrs Hemmings to prepare a bath.'

He looked down at his soot-stained clothes and grimaced. In his hurry to leave London he had packed light, but both his shirts had ended up grimy after the day spent fighting the tavern fire.

'Thank you.'

Alice nodded, holding his eye for just a second, and then she turned to leave.

'Alice,' he said, closing the space between them. 'Wait.'

As she spun to face him, he saw the sadness in her eyes and hated that he was the cause of it.

'Forgive me,' he said, his words quiet but clear. 'Please forgive me.'

There was a flare of something conciliatory in Alice's eyes, and then she looked away. 'I don't know if I can,' she said quietly. Without any fuss and without looking at him again, she walked away.

Chapter Twenty-Two

Alice had the urge to walk out of the house and keep walking. She wanted her face to be whipped by the wind, her hair flying loose about her shoulders and her skirt battering her legs. There was nothing quite like the wind as it hit the dunes on this part of the coast, and she felt the need to feel the cleansing sting as it brought colour to her cheeks.

She had not made any promises to listen to what Simon had to say, although she knew at some point they would need to discuss the future. They were still married: nothing could change that. It was only Alice's hopes and dreams and expectations that had changed.

Before she could change her mind, she grabbed her bonnet from its place close to the door, secured it tightly under her chin and then slipped out of the grand house. There was a path through the grounds that led to a narrow lane, and a twenty-minute brisk walk would bring her to the beach.

It had been a shock to see Simon so soon after she had arrived back in Northumberland, less than a day after she and Maria had pulled up in the carriage. Maria had reiterated her invitation to Alice to stay with her, but in the end Alice had decided she wanted a few days alone. She felt as though she were in mourning, experiencing a sadness for the loss of the dream she had woven around their lives.

Now with Simon back, she did not know what to think. He must have left London soon after they had and raced up here to speak to her, but that did not mean anything had changed—not really.

As Alice stepped onto the sand, she felt a powerful sense of being home. She loved London, loved the crowds and the sense that there was always something going on, but Northumberland was where she felt she belonged.

She climbed over the low dunes and walked along the beach a little, pleased to see she had the wide expanse of sand to herself. It was hardly weather for the beach, with the wind whipping up the sand every now and then so that she had to shield her eyes.

She chose a spot near the dunes where she was sheltered from the worst of the wind and made herself comfortable. What she loved most up here was the wide expanse of the sea. The water was always dark, the sand golden white, the sky changing with the seasons, yet one thing that never changed was the horizon. When she looked along the beach in either direction, as far as the eye could see was the flat line of the sea on the horizon, as if beckoning her to new adventures.

Alice sat for a long time, trying not to think of anything.

'I thought I might find you out here,' Simon said, surprising her. She hadn't thought he would follow her down to the beach.

He looked much fresher now after a bath, the soot washed from him and the grime scrubbed from his hair.

'I like the solitude on the beach, that sense that you are the only person in the whole world when you look out to sea.'

'It is beautiful.'

'Was your journey too strenuous?'

'It was not the most straightforward.'

'Was that soot on your clothing?'

'An inn I was staying at caught fire. I stayed to help put out the flames, but it was an old timber building, and the fire was relentless.'

Alice's eyes widened. 'Were you hurt?'

'No. Thankfully, no one was. The fire started when the innkeeper was cooking breakfast, so most of the guests were up, and there was time to rouse those who were not.'

'Did it spread to the rest of the village?'

'No.'

'That is something.' Alice shuddered. 'I always had such a fear of fire when I was a child. I used to fall asleep scared one of our neighbours would leave a candle burning and the whole row of houses would go up in flames.'

'I had never before seen a fire like this one. It was a destructive force, ripping through the building at such a speed you cannot imagine. It felt as though one minute there was a building with four walls and a roof, the next it was just a collection of timber supports left, sticking up from the ground with nothing to hold onto them.'

'I am glad you were not harmed,' Alice said, fixing her gaze again on the horizon.

He placed his hand on the sand next to hers, and Alice

felt the familiar spark travel through her as his finger brushed against hers.

'How are you? Has your wound completely healed?'

'It still pulls a little when I walk quickly, but apart from that it seems well healed.'

'I am glad.' He paused and then pressed on. 'I am sorry, Alice. Leaving you like that was unforgiveable.'

She shrugged, not meeting his eye. 'I should not be so upset. I should have expected it.'

'No,' he said sharply. 'I do not want you to expect such a thing.'

She turned to him, tears in her eyes. 'In London, after I had been injured, I thought that maybe something had changed between us, that maybe there was a chance that you could love me.'

There was pain in his eyes in response to her words, and he pressed his lips together so hard they went completely white. She realised how close he was to losing control and tentatively laid a hand over his. No matter how much she was hurting, she did not want to see Simon suffer like this. He had suffered enough in the last twenty years to last a lifetime.

'Can I tell you something? I know I have no right, but can I ask for your indulgence one last time before you decide what you are going to do?' He spoke quietly, but Alice could see he had control of himself again.

'Yes.'

'For twenty-one years I have been in mourning, but for the past five years I have felt as though I do not deserve to be here. I have hated every step I have had to take in Robert's shoes, every one of his duties I have had to shoulder. I have felt unworthy, and it has drained my very soul.'

Alice saw the anguish in his eyes and realised how much he had been suffering. She wanted to fold him in her arms and kiss him until he forgot the darkness, despite everything they had been through, but she knew he had to get this out in the open. Only then might he be able to begin to heal.

'Added to that is the fear that I will be struck down by the same condition that killed my father and my brother. I didn't want to die, didn't want my life to be over, but I felt like it was inevitable given how two good men, *better* men, had already been taken.'

'Not better,' Alice murmured.

'I have been hiding away, scared of dying but not feeling worthy of the life I had. The only way I knew how to cope was to push people away. Then I met you.' He flicked a glance at her, and she gave him an encouraging smile. 'That night at the Midsummer's Eve ball, when I met you I felt something shift. I was happy for the first time in a long time. It was as though you wakened something inside me.' He shook his head ruefully. 'Then I reverted back to my old ways and ran away, thinking I was sparing everyone the pain I felt, not realising I was only causing more of it.'

He turned to her, and Alice gave him an encouraging nod. She could feel the tears running down her cheeks as the wind whipped at them, but she didn't wipe them away.

'When I returned I did not know how we would live as husband and wife, but as soon as I saw you again I began falling in love. I fell hard and fast, even as I tried to pretend I felt nothing.'

Alice felt her eyes widen. She hadn't expected him to be able to say he loved her. For the first time since he had arrived in Northumberland, she allowed her mind to begin racing, to wonder if perhaps they had a chance at a future.

'You were like a magic potion, Alice. As you drew me in I started to realise little by little how terrible I had been feeling, how badly I had been treating myself, and how badly I had treated you. It was liberating to allow myself pleasure, to seek out enjoyment in things and realise that the guilt I was feeling for surviving when my brother had not was irrational. You did all of that. You showed me what it was to love and be loved.'

He reached out and stroked her cheek, and Alice felt a warmth flood through her body. She wanted to kiss him, to embrace him, but she knew it was important he say everything he needed to.

'When you were stabbed, I felt as though my world were ending. I didn't know how I would cope without you, even though I could not admit it to myself. I got so scared at the thought of losing someone else I loved. I tried to push everything down, to deny what I was feeling. Then when that man approached us in the street, mistaking me for Robert, it was as if every worry from the past came crashing back. I was overwhelmed. Suddenly I felt like a fraud, as if all the progress I had made was not real.' He shook his head. 'I am so sorry for abandoning you then, Alice. It was the worst possible thing I could have done.'

'Where did you go?'

'I walked the streets for hours, and then the next morning I went up the Monument. It was a place I used to visit with my father when I was young, and I realised I needed to properly clear my head, properly address what had happened.'

'That was when you came up with all of this?'

'It was the start. The journey here gave me a lot of time to think as well.'

Alice fell silent, her fingers drawing patterns in the sand by her sides.

'And now?' she asked eventually.

'Now I throw myself on your mercy, Alice. I love you with all my heart. Your smile lights up my world, and your laughter soothes my soul. I will do anything in my power to make you happy every day for the rest of our lives.'

'You want us to live as husband and wife?'

'Yes. More than anything.'

Alice felt her heart jump in her chest. Nothing was certain in life, but her main fear of giving her heart to Simon was that he would one day soon abandon her again. Now that he had acknowledged the reasons for his actions these past few years, she doubted he would act in the same way.

'I love you, Simon. I fell in love with you on the night of the Midsummer's Eve ball, and I have been pining for you ever since.'

'Do you think you can give me another chance?'

Alice closed her eyes and thought of all the reasons it might not work, then pushed them away. She loved him and he loved her. That was all they needed. Anything else they could work through together.

'Yes,' she said, leaning forward and kissing him.

'I have a question for you, one I hope you will say *yes* to.'

She frowned, puzzled.

Carefully he took something out of his jacket pocket and held it up so the light glinted off it. 'Alice, will you do me the honour of continuing to be my wife?'

'Is that my ring?'

'Yes.'

'How did you get it back?'

'The scoundrel who stabbed you was caught and brought before the magistrate a few days later. It seems he was wanted for a whole string of crimes. I talked to the magistrate, and they allowed me to search his possessions. He still had the ring on him when he was arrested.' He held it out. 'I will understand if you wish to have a different ring. We can choose one that does not have such memories associated with it.'

'No,' Alice said quickly. 'That is my wedding ring. That is the ring you placed on my finger when we married.'

Simon smiled and carefully slipped it onto the ring finger of her left hand.

'My beautiful wife,' he murmured and then leaned in and kissed her.

The wind whipped Alice's hair about her face, and the sand coated her skin, but Alice barely noticed. She was lost in the kiss of the man she loved, the man she had fallen for that very first night she had met him on a magical Midsummer's Eve.

Epilogue

❧

Northumberland, Midsummer's Eve, 1818

Alice adjusted her mask, ensuring the ribbons were tied securely behind her head, and then she stepped out into the middle of the ballroom. The guests had been arriving for the last half an hour, and now Westcroft Hall was filled with chatter and laughter and music. Most people were wearing masks, delicate demimasks that barely concealed their identities, but it added to the sense of excitement.

'Good evening,' came a low voice from behind her, and Alice spun, a shiver running down her spine. Simon was standing there, dressed in a black jacket and gold cravat, easily the most handsome man in the room. 'May I have this dance?'

Alice inclined her head, and they walked to the dance floor to share the first dance of the evening.

Everyone was watching, but for Alice it felt as though they were the only two there, twirling around the ballroom as they did when they were the only two people in residence. For the duration of the dance she gazed into

Simon's eyes, and even as the music swelled and then died away, she found it hard to tear herself away.

'You're going to tell me I cannot have the next dance with you now, aren't you?' Simon said, a smile tugging at his lips.

Alice leaned in closer. 'If it were up to me, I would dance every single one with you, but we must fulfil our duties as host and hostess.'

'Can I tell you a secret?' Simon said, leaning in so his lips brushed against her ear.

Alice nodded.

'I would be willing to be labelled the worst host in the history of society balls if it meant I got to spend my evening only with you.'

'That is hardly a secret,' Alice said. She had the urge to kiss him and found her body swaying towards him.

'*Everyone* is watching,' Maria said as she glided over gracefully. 'If you ravish your wife here in the middle of the dance floor, you will never be able to show your faces in society again.'

'I would never,' Simon said, his eyes still locked on Alice's. 'A mere kiss, however…'

Alice felt helpless to resist and even began rising up on tiptoes until Maria gripped her arm.

'I am borrowing your wife, Simon. I'll give her back to you once you are no longer the centre of attention.'

Maria slipped her arm through Alice's and led her from the dance floor.

'This is marvellous, Alice. The most incredible ball I have ever been to.' Alice flushed with pleasure. It had been Simon's idea to host a ball on Midsummer's Eve, two years from the date they had first met, but Alice had been the one to remember all the details that had made the last ball so special and then to add in many more of her own.

The ballroom was beautifully decorated with fresh flowers spilling out of vases on tables and plinths around the room. Candles twinkled in the chandelier above their heads and in the sconces around the walls. It made the whole room look like a magical faerie glade, and their guests had embraced this theme with the women wearing floaty, flowery dresses and even some of the men tucking a rosebud or similar boutonnière.

The ballroom was not the only room that was decorated. They had decided on a woodland theme for each area, and it meant the entrance hall had garlands of leaves strung about it in a criss-cross pattern, making it look like their guests were entering the house under a canopy of trees. They had also opened up the drawing room as a quieter, cooler alternative to the ballroom, and for here Alice had sourced dozens of ferns that gave the room a calming atmosphere.

'The girls begged me to let them come and see the room decorated and everyone in their masks,' Maria said as they made their way through the crowd of people. 'I brought them down a little earlier, and I think Sylvia is convinced you are some sort of magical creature, placed in our family to bring us good luck.'

Alice flushed. The past year had flown by, and she and Simon had split their time between London and Northumberland, but by far her favourite part was spending time with their beautiful nieces.

She placed a hand on her swollen belly, looking down anxiously for a moment. They had discussed the subject of children of their own again and again in the early days after Simon's return. Simon worried about passing on whatever his father and brother had died from to any child of his, but as time passed he had also acknowledged that this was another unknown, something that might never come to pass, very much like his own risk of sudden death. They had agreed to put the subject to one side for a year or two and focus on the charity work Alice spent much of her time devoted to and touring the Westcroft properties to ensure everything was in order after Simon's long period away. They had continued to find it difficult to keep their hands off one another, but they took precautions. Fate had another idea, and a few months earlier Alice had realised she was pregnant.

In a way it had been better happening like this, the decision taken out of their hands. It was no one's fault, no one's decision, and as Alice's belly grew, their excitement for starting a family of their own did too.

They had returned to Northumberland a month earlier to prepare for the Midsummer's Eve ball and now planned to stay here until well after Alice had given birth. Alice wanted the reassurance of Maria's presence, and also she felt less nauseous when she could breathe in the fresh sea air rather than the heavy odours of London. Her own sister was planning on making the long journey up from Devon in a few months so she could also be on hand, which would also allow Alice to spend some precious time with Margaret and her little son.

They moved from group to group, exchanging pleasantries with their friends and neighbours, until Alice heard the first notes of a waltz and felt a hand on her shoulder.

'You promised me this dance, my love,' Simon said, his voice low and seductive.

This time he led her not to the dance floor but to the terrace beyond where there were lamps set along the stone balustrade and couples strolled arm-in-arm. They had been blessed with perfect weather for their ball. There was not a cloud in the sky, and hundreds of stars twinkled, helping to illuminate the terrace and the gardens beyond. Simon pulled her close, placing one had in the small of her back, and then they fell into step. Alice's heart soared as he twirled her and caught her and guided her across the terrace. When they danced like this, it always felt as though their bodies moved as one, perfectly synchronised like two swans gliding across a calm lake. As with the ball two years earlier, they had quite the audience by the time they had finished dancing, but everyone looked on indulgently, seeing nothing more than a young married couple enjoying the first flush of wedded bliss.

'This is the part where I should lead you into the garden,' Simon said, leaning close so his lips were almost touching hers.

'I think that might raise a few eyebrows.'

'You're right. Perhaps I should do this instead.'

He grinned at her and then closed the distance between them, brushing his lips against her own. The kiss was passionate but brief, even Simon knew he could not seduce his wife in front of sixty of the wealthiest and most influential people in Northumberland.

'This ball is perfect,' Alice said, rising up on her toes to whisper in his ear. 'But now I cannot wait for it to finish so we can retire upstairs.'

As Simon took her hand in his own, Alice rested her head against his shoulder and looked up at the stars, enjoying the perfect moment on a perfect night.

* * * * *